W9-ALN-143

DISCARD
WEST GEORGIA REGIONAL LIBRARY SYSTEM
Neva Lomason Memorial Library

GHOSTS *in the* FAMILY

also by MARILYN SACHS

MARILYN SACHS

GHOSTS
in the
FAMILY

Dutton Children's Books • New York

Copyright © 1995 by Marilyn Sachs

All rights reserved. No part of this publication may be reproduced or
transmitted in any form or by any means, electronic or mechanical,
including photocopy, recording, or any information storage and retrieval
system now known or to be invented, without permission in writing
from the publisher, except by a reviewer who wishes to quote brief
passages in connection with a review written for inclusion in a
magazine, newspaper, or broadcast.

Library of Congress Cataloging-in-Publication Data
Sachs, Marilyn.
Ghosts in the family / by Marilyn Sachs.—1st ed.
p. cm.
Summary: Eleven-year-old Gabriella learns some unpleasant truths
about her often-absent father and his relationship with her
and her Mexican mother.
ISBN 0-525-45421-7
[1. Fathers and daughters—Fiction. 2. Family problems—Fiction.
3. Aunts—Fiction. 4. Mexican Americans—Fiction.] I. Title.
PZ7.S1187Gh 1995
[Fic]—dc20 94-36992 CIP AC

Published in the United States by Dutton Children's Books,
a division of Penguin Books USA Inc.
375 Hudson Street, New York, New York 10014

Editor: Ann Durell
Designer: Semadar Megged
Printed in USA
First Edition
1 3 5 7 9 10 8 6 4 2

For my youngest grandchild (so far), the dazzling "Queena" Lena— with love and amazement

GHOSTS *in the* FAMILY

1

"NO! NO! GHOSTS AREN'T REAL. No! Why do you tell her such things?" Mami always got angry at Papi when he told me how the ghost of Gabriel Valencia appeared to him that one time when he was suffering.

"Because it's true, Estela. You remember. I told you so then."

"You were upset," Mami cried. "It was a bad dream —a nightmare." I could tell Mami was frightened. No matter what she said, I knew she believed in ghosts, too.

"It wasn't a nightmare, Estela, because I wasn't a bit afraid," Papi said. "Maybe I would have been afraid if it had been a bad ghost."

"Shh! Shh!" Mami said. "Don't say things like that."

"But this was a good ghost, Gabriella"—Papi nodded at the portrait—"and he gave me the courage to go on."

THE PORTRAIT HAD HUNG IN MY BEDROOM FOR AS LONG as I could remember. His name was Gabriel Valencia, my great-great-great-great-great-grandfather, and I was named for him. In the picture he was only a boy, but he would grow up, Papi said, to be a great man, the *comandante* of the old Presidio here in San Francisco, when it was occupied by the Spanish. I was lucky, Papi said, to be descended from such a great man.

I liked to wake up in the morning and see him there, watching over me.

"He looks at me," I told Papi. "Even when I get up and move around the room, his eyes follow me."

Papi laughed. "I thought so too when I was a child. It's a trick the painter used."

The boy in the painting was dark-haired and dark-eyed, just as I was. He didn't look anything at all like my blond, blue-eyed father. He wore a uniform, and on his hand was a gold ring.

"The same one you're wearing," Papi said. "It's come down through all the generations and is given to the first child born in the new generation—boy or girl."

Papi said that when the ghost came and stood next to his bed, it reached out and touched Papi's ring finger with its own.

"Of course, the ring hasn't fit me since I grew up, but in my dream I was still wearing it, and so was he."

"But weren't you frightened, Papi?" I asked, shivering and snuggling up to him. I loved hearing about the ghost, especially safe on Papi's lap with his arms around me.

"No, I wasn't," Papi said. "Not at all. Before he came, I was frightened because I was so confused. I knew I was making my family miserable, and I knew your mother was miserable, and, Gabriella, I tell you honestly, I didn't know if I could even live through it all."

Papi always talked to me like a grown-up, especially when Mami wasn't around. Usually, he told me about the ghost when we were alone. He didn't like to upset Mami.

"But, Papi, what did it feel like when he touched your hand? Was it cold and bony like a skeleton's?"

"No, Gabriella, it was like a surge of courage. Like strength flowing through my veins. He didn't say anything. He just touched my ring with his, and I could feel the strength coming back to me, the courage flowing through me. I knew he was telling me to be brave, the way he always had, and to do the right thing."

The right thing was to marry Mami even though his mother and sister, who were rich and lived in a great, big, grand house, would disinherit him and throw him out just because Mami was poor and from Mexico.

"I only wish," Papi said, "that I could have given her an easier life. She deserves it. She doesn't deserve to work so hard and struggle so."

"She doesn't struggle, Papi. She loves cooking, and . . ."

"She's always tired, and we never have enough money. I try my best, but . . ." Sometimes Papi's eyes would fill up with tears. And then I would tell him how happy Mami was, and how happy I was, and how lucky I felt to have such a handsome, kind, wonderful man like Papi for my father.

I LOVED HEARING MAMI AND PAPI TALK ABOUT HOW THEY met when Mami was a waitress at the El Niño restaurant.

"Tell me again how he came in, and he didn't know you yet," I begged.

"Well, he was doing an article on Mexican food for some newspaper," Mami said.

"No, Estela, it was for *Holiday Magazine*. They didn't take it, and eventually, I did sell it to the *San Rafael Reporter.*"

"Oh, well, I saw him sitting there." Mami shook her head, smiling. "He was . . . well . . . so good-looking . . . like . . . like . . . Robert Redford. He didn't see me."

"Now, Estela, how can you say that. I saw you as soon as I came in. I pretended to be looking at the sombreros on the wall, but I kept watching you. You were so pretty, the prettiest little . . ."

Mami giggled and shook her head even harder. "So, Gabriella, there he was. He was interviewing Mr. Rojas, the owner, and I waited on his table. But then . . ." Mami turned her head to one side and laughed out loud. "But then, I tripped, and the tortillas fell on Mr. Rojas's head."

"And the soup went all over, and some of it splashed on Mr. Rojas," I continued happily. "And then Papi jumped up, and—"

"No, no," Papi said, laughing. "First I just tried to mop him up. My God, he was a mess. She really got him good."

"But then you said, 'It's my fault, Mr. Rojas. She tripped on my foot,' but . . ."

"It didn't make any difference," Mami said. "Mr. Rojas just fired me right on the spot."

"And then Papi waited for you afterward."

"And . . . and . . ." Mami sighed. ". . . And one thing led to another, and . . ."

"And . . ." Papi took her hand. "And we fell in love, and got married, and lived happily ever after."

Mami sighed.

"Except you didn't get a bargain, Estela, did you?" Papi said, gently pressing Mami's head down on his shoulder.

"No, no, Philip, I did. Of course I did."

"You got a liability when you married me, and now you have to work twice as hard."

"But Mami," I said, "you left out how Papi encouraged you to get a job in another restaurant, and you learned to cook, and . . ."

"I always knew how to cook," Mami said angrily. "But because I'm a woman, and because they know they can always pay me less . . . like now, I can make the same dishes the chef makes, only he gets paid twice as much." Mami worked now as an assistant chef for El Toreador restaurant.

"One day, Estela," Papi said, "I'll make it big, and then you'll be able to stay home. I'll write my book, and we'll be rolling in the money."

"I'm not complaining, Philip," Mami said.

"I know you're not," said Papi. "You never complain even when you should. But, believe me, Estela, one day soon, it's all going to come together."

2.

OF COURSE MAMI DID COMPLAIN. At night, in their bedroom, when they thought I was asleep and couldn't hear.

"Why not?" Mami asked in her quick, hurt voice. "Why not?"

"It doesn't work out, Estela, that's why," Papi said patiently. He never raised his voice to Mami or to me either. "When I'm home I like to be alone with you and Gabriella."

"No, Philip, it's because you're ashamed, that's why. You're ashamed for your fancy friends to meet me and see how we live. That's why."

"Estela! Estela!"

"Never," Mami insisted. "You never invite anybody here, but you always go to their houses. You always go by yourself, and you . . ."

"It's business, Estela. I don't do it for pleasure. It's not a pleasure, believe me. . . . You wouldn't enjoy yourself. And I always ask you to come. You know I do, Estela."

"Oh, you ask me, but I know you really don't want me along. But anyway, you always complain about the bad food."

"Can you blame me, Estela? I'm spoiled by you. Nobody cooks like you. But my darling girl, if you're unhappy, I'll bring people home. Most of them are boring, but I'll try to think of some you can stand."

"When, Philip? Just give me a little time, and I'll cook your friends a meal they'll never forget."

"I know, darling, I know. Well, not this time. I'll be leaving the day after tomorrow, but next time I'm home. Next time for sure."

I ALWAYS TRIED MY BEST TO BE THE KIND OF PERSON PAPI and Gabriel Valencia wanted me to be. Whenever Papi was around, I tried to be polite and happy and respectful, but when he wasn't around, it was hard for me to keep it up.

"It's your fault! It's your fault!" I yelled at Mami the day after I'd heard their conversation. Papi wasn't home.

"Now, Gabriella, *mamacita*, just calm down and listen . . ."

"I won't listen! You always pick on Papi. That's why he goes away so much. You keep nagging him and nagging him about his friends, and . . ."

"Listen, *mamacita*, listen . . ."

"I won't! I won't!" I dropped down on the floor and kicked my feet up and down and howled. I knew I was being unfair to Mami. I also wanted Papi to bring his friends home and was angry and ashamed that he didn't. But I couldn't say it that way. The only way I could say it was to fall down on the floor and kick my feet up and down. Mami always picked me up and held me until I calmed down. By the time Papi came home, I was smiling and polite again.

Mami hardly ever complained about Papi or about me. But she did complain about Tía Nicolasa. Tía Nicolasa lived next door in our building and looked after me when Mami worked. She wasn't really my aunt, but she and my mother had been friends from a long time ago. Mami always said Tía Nicolasa was her best friend, but she complained about her more than about anybody else except for Mr. Peralta, her boss.

"Just because we're friends doesn't mean she can tell me how to live my life."

"She's so bossy, Mami. You should hear how she talks to Tío Raúl."

"I know," Mami said. "And she thinks just because her husband puts up with all her nagging I should treat my husband the same way."

"She's always talking about Papi," I told her. "She asks me lots of questions, and she always wants to know why his friends don't come over."

"I'm going to tell her off once and for all," Mami said, jumping up.

"BECAUSE HE'S NOT HOME THAT MUCH, AND WHEN HE IS," Mami said angrily, "he wants to be with Gabriella and me. If he goes out himself, it's always on business. Of course he always asks me, but I never want to go. I don't like what you keep implying, Nicolasa."

Tía Nicolasa spread out her hands. "Did I ever say anything to you? Did I?"

"Well, not about that. But you ask Gabriella. I know. Gabriella told me you did."

Tía Nicolasa narrowed her eyes at me. She had a quick temper, and she used it on Tío Raúl, María Dolores, Manuel, and even sometimes on me.

"Gabriella is a spoiled brat!" Tía Nicolasa snapped. "You spoil her, and you spoil him."

"Ah!" Mami nodded and looked hard at her. "So, now it all comes out."

"It's not the first time I've said so. You let Gabriella

get away with all those temper tantrums of hers, and you never expect her to pick up after herself. And as for him . . ." Tía Nicolasa took a few deep breaths to calm herself down. "Listen, Estela, you know I care for you. You're my oldest friend. You're like my sister. You know I want the best for you."

Mami didn't answer, but she turned her eyes away from Tía Nicolasa's face.

Tía Nicolasa patted her belly. "You know, Estela, if this baby is a girl, I'm going to name her Estela. And I want you to be her godmother."

"I know. I know," said my mother, "but you get me so angry sometimes, Nicolasa. Why can't you just see that I'm very happy and that my husband is wonderful to me and to Gabriella."

Tía Nicolasa made a choky, muffled sound.

"He's an artist," Mami insisted. "He writes beautiful articles about places I never even heard of. It's not his fault if . . . but, Nicolasa, he did have a book published once, and he tries. . . . One of these days, he says, he knows he's going to make it big."

"He's got a family," Tía Nicolasa said carefully. "Most men, if they have a family, they get a job, even if it's not exactly what they want. You think Raúl wants to be working day and night at the service station? Don't you remember, Estela, how he used to play in the band when we were young? And how we used to go hear him, and how we all loved to dance? Don't you remember?"

"Yes," Mami said. "I remember."

TÍO RAÚL OWNED A SERVICE STATION ON MISSION STREET. He and Tía Nicolasa were saving money to buy their own house. She stayed home with her kids, María Dolores and Manuel. And she took care of me while Mami worked. I never had tantrums with Tía Nicolasa. I didn't dare.

Tío Raúl said Tía Nicolasa was like a tinderbox because she had such a quick temper. Mostly she used it on her own family.

"Turn off the TV, María Dolores, and get over here and do your homework! Gabriella is almost finished with hers."

"It's too hard," María Dolores said. She was eleven, just like me, and in my class at school. She wasn't one of the good students, and Tía Nicolasa was always yelling at her.

"Well, you just sit down and do it anyway," Tía Nicolasa snapped. "If you don't understand something, you can ask me or Gabriella. I don't know why I have to nag you so much. I never have to nag Gabriella or Manuel. That's why they both get such good marks."

"Manuel is only in second grade. It's easy in second grade."

"That's not what you said in second grade," said her mother. "Now *sit!*"

María Dolores made a face, but she joined me at the kitchen table and opened her math book.

Sometimes Tía Nicolasa would talk to me about how she and Mami used to have fun before they married. She said Mami always loved to go shopping and buy clothes for herself.

"She hardly ever buys any clothes for herself now," I said. "Mami says most of the time all she needs at work is a clean apron."

"I remember once she had a beautiful blue flare skirt with a blouse that matched, only it had pink and white flowers in the front. And she wore a pink flower in her hair, the same color as the flowers in the blouse. It really was beautiful," Tía Nicolasa said. "She really knew how to dress up."

"She likes to buy clothes for me now or sometimes for Papi."

Tía Nicolasa liked to talk about what a devoted husband Tío Raúl was and how hard he worked. She said she was lucky to have a husband like Tío Raúl, and then she would start in talking about our family.

"It's a shame your mother has to work so hard."

"She doesn't mind," I told her. "She likes to cook, but she thinks the boss should pay her more."

"She has no time for herself and never enough

money. If she had sense, she would tell your papi that he had to pull his weight a little more and help out with the finances. But she never thinks of herself."

"My papi is going to make it big one day," I told her. "Mami knows that and so do I."

Tía Nicolasa narrowed her eyes at me and said, "Now I don't want you to go and tell your mother what I just said. You tell her everything. You're a real blabbermouth."

"I won't," I promised.

BUT I DID. I TOLD MAMI WHAT SHE SAID, AND MAMI GOT angry and complained. I always told Mami everything except what Papi said about the ghost or the way he raised his eyebrows.

3.

WHENEVER MAMI HAD A DAY OFF, if Papi was away, she always tried to clean up the house fast so she could spend time with me. Sometimes we went shopping for clothes—for me or for Papi. Sometimes, if there was money, we went to a movie, but most of the time, we just took walks together and window-shopped.

Sometimes Mami took me to look at my Grandmother Russell's house. Although it wasn't far away, it was on a beautiful, tree-lined street, nothing like the street where I lived. It was a great big house, the one my father had grown up in and where my grandmother and aunt still lived.

"I wasn't good enough for his mother." Mami's teeth were clenched. "She wouldn't even meet me—or you either. She thinks her family's so great, but they all came from Mexico, too, just like me."

"From Spain, Mami. Papi says they came from Spain. He says Gabriel Valencia's family were important people in Spain."

"She wouldn't meet me—all right, she wouldn't meet me! But you—her one and only grandchild! And I know if she saw you—just for one second—for one second—she would have to be overjoyed. It's not natural."

I thought so, too. I used to daydream about Grandmother Russell. About how she would meet me somewhere accidentally. And how she would wrinkle up her face when she saw mine. How she would step forward and ask my name. How she would start crying when she learned who I was. And then . . . she would throw her arms around me and beg my forgiveness.

"But, Mami, why don't we just call her up and tell her we want to meet her?"

"No, no! She'd never agree. She wanted him to marry a rich society girl, not somebody like me. She threw him out, and her daughter—your aunt—Papi's sister—it was really her fault, Papi says. She was always jealous of him. She put her mother up to it. She told her lies about me."

How I hated my aunt! In my daydreams, after my grandmother had begged my forgiveness, and begged my father's forgiveness, and my mother's, after that, after she had welcomed us to her house, she would turn on my aunt. I could see my grandmother as a beautiful old lady who looked like Papi. I couldn't see my aunt clearly, but I knew she had a mean, ugly face. I liked to imagine how my grandmother would order my aunt out of the house and slam the door behind her.

Mami and I always watched from across the street. There was a gardener who clipped the hedges in front of the house. Once we watched two painters repaint the house gray and black.

"You'd think they could come up with prettier colors," Mami said. "If it was my house, I would paint it maybe yellow with blue trim."

"How about pink, Mami, with sort of purple trim?" I suggested.

"Yes, that would be nice, too. Anything would be better than gray and black."

Another time, we watched a window washer on a scaffold, washing all of the windows.

"You want to guess how much that costs—to have somebody wash your windows?"

"I don't know, Mami. You always wash the windows in our apartment."

"Hundreds of dollars it must cost," Mami said bitterly. "And not a penny for their own flesh and blood."

"It's such a big house, Mami," I said. "Isn't it too big for just two people?"

"That's the way rich people live, *mi'ja*—not like us poor slobs in our little apartment, but one day . . ."

She went on to say that one day when Papi made it big we would buy our own house. But in my daydreams, Grandmother Russell would fling open the doors and welcome us into her house. It would be a fancy house with beautiful furniture and great big tables full of china dishes and big candlesticks like the rich houses we saw on TV.

PAPI RAISED HIS EYEBROWS SOMETIMES WHEN MAMI AND Tía Nicolasa talked together. Usually when Papi was home, Tía Nicolasa kept away. But every so often, if she had to come by to drop off some clothes I'd left in her apartment, Papi would ask her to sit down and have a cup of coffee.

"No! No!" she would protest. "I'm in a big hurry. I have to go."

She always had to go somewhere when Papi was home.

Sometimes he would insist. And Mami would insist. Then Tía Nicolasa would sit down carefully on the chair as if it had scorpions on it, smile politely at Papi, say hardly anything, drink her coffee quickly, and leave.

Sometimes she forgot to leave quickly. Maybe Mami

had a funny story to tell about one of the customers in her restaurant, or maybe one of the neighbors had shared some interesting piece of gossip with her. Sometimes Tía Nicolasa might forget my father was there. Sometimes she and my mother might both forget, and then they would laugh and talk, just the two of them, for a few minutes. Sometimes they spoke in Spanish.

That's when my father's eyebrows rose. He would smile and look at me and raise his eyebrows. And I would smile back and raise my eyebrows. It was our own special little joke, and I never told my mother. Mami and I sometimes spoke to each other in Spanish, but never when he was around.

THE NIGHT BEFORE HE LEFT, MY FATHER SAT WITH ME BEfore I went to bed, talking about Gabriel Valencia.

"He grew up to be the most famous *comandante* of the Presidio. Everybody loved him and admired him. The good padres who ran the mission said they could not have survived without him. He drove off the pirates who sailed up and down the coast, terrorizing the settlers. He helped the Indians improve their miserable lives, and they loved him. When he brought his bride to San Francisco, they strewed flowers in her path."

Papi stopped to smile.

"Go on, Papi! Go on!"

"He was a very great man, Gabriella, which is why I named you after him. He had a hard life, but he was always brave and good. It takes courage; you have to remember that, Gabriella. And I hope you'll grow up to be just like him."

"Yes, Papi, I'll try."

Papi bent over to kiss me. "You're a good girl, Gabriella, and I'm going to miss you and Mami very much."

"Oh, Papi," I cried, "I wish you didn't have to go. It's so lonely when you're gone. Please, Papi, don't go."

"I have to go," Papi said, stroking my hair. His face grew serious. "This time, Gabriella, it's a little different. I'm finally going to start writing my big book on modern exploration. Believe it or not, there are still places all over the world nobody has ever described. And I'm going to be the one who does. This time, I know I'm going to set the publishing world on its ear, and I'll make a killing."

"Please, Papi!"

"But it will go fast, maybe a few months at the most, and then we'll be together again."

I clung to him, smelling his good, clean, after-shave smell. Then I started crying. Papi didn't like it when I cried, but this time he picked me up in his arms and hugged me tight.

"Promise me," he said, "you'll take good care of Mami and do whatever she tells you."

"I promise," I told him.

"And I want you to be brave. I want you to remember Gabriel Valencia." He pushed my chin up, and I stopped crying.

"Yes, Papi," I told him. "I will."

4

USUALLY WHEN MY FATHER TRAVELED, he sent me picture postcards. I saved them all and liked to show them to my friends. Sometimes my teachers asked me to show them to the whole class and tell the kids about all the different countries my father had visited.

"You show off too much," María Dolores said.

María Dolores had lots of friends at school. Everybody liked her, even though she kidded around a lot and wasn't one of the smartest kids in the class. I was one of the smartest kids, but not everybody liked me.

"It's because you keep showing off," María Dolores said. "That's why. You go on and on about how great your father is and what a great family you're descended from."

"Well, it's true."

"I'm just telling you what the other kids say." María Dolores grinned at me. "I don't know about great or not great, but you're real lucky to have your father always off traveling. I wish mine would go travel somewhere, too. I wish both my parents would travel and stop picking on me. They never pick on Manuel."

She and I got along pretty well. I often helped her with her homework, and she generally stuck up for me when other kids made fun of me.

Teachers liked me. Ms. González, my fifth-grade teacher, was always telling the other kids in my class how smart I was, and how I always did my homework and sometimes even more than I had to do, and that she knew I was going to grow up to be the kind of person everybody would be very proud of. She also said that if more of the kids took their schoolwork seriously, as I did, they could also become excellent students. I felt proud when Ms. González talked to the kids in my class about me, but it didn't make them like me any better.

BUT THIS TIME NO POSTCARDS CAME. I CHECKED OUR MAIL-box at least twice a day, but no postcards came.

"Why isn't Papi writing?" I asked Mami.

Mami looked worried. "It's different this time," she said. "You know he's starting his big book, and he needs to spend a lot of time thinking."

"Thinking? Isn't Papi always thinking?"

"Well, yes, Gabriella, he is. But this time it's sort of special. . . . He'll be writing a new kind of book about modern exploration and—well, I'm not sure what else. He's starting out in Tibet, and the mail comes very slowly from such a faraway place. Don't worry. I'm sure he's fine. There's nothing to worry about."

I knew she worried. Sometimes at night I could hear her crying. I worried, too, and I wished that some postcards would come—just one postcard at least.

But I didn't cry. Whenever I felt like crying, I thought about Gabriel Valencia and looked at his picture—at the stern-faced boy with my gold ring on the middle finger of his left hand—my gold ring with the two tiny serpents entwined around each other. I turned it on my own finger and could almost feel a surge of the courage Papi talked about. Yes, I would be brave like Gabriel Valencia and like my father.

The ring was beginning to feel tight, and I knew I would have to move it one day soon to my ring finger. I wondered if Gabriel Valencia had moved it to his ring finger when it grew too tight on him.

TÍA NICOLASA'S BABY WAS BORN—A GIRL. SHE WAS NAMED Estela, and my mother held her in the church when she was baptized. We all had fun that day. We had a party with wonderful food that my Mami had cooked. Nobody could cook like Mami.

BUT NO POSTCARDS CAME.

"I talked to the postman," Mami said. "He told me it can take months for letters and cards to come from Tibet. He said sometimes they get lost and that we shouldn't worry." Mami tried to smile. "It's important for Papi to have this time that he needs to start his book. I suppose he has so much on his mind, he just forgets to write to us. I'm sure we'll hear from him <u>soon</u>."

THE CHEF AT EL TOREADOR QUIT, AND THE NEW CHEF WAS slow in learning the ropes. Mr. Peralta asked Mami to help out until he did. She had to work longer and longer hours, and she began to have bags under her eyes. She wanted me to sleep over at Tía Nicolasa's house because some nights she didn't get home until after midnight.

I refused. Now that I was eleven, I felt I could look after myself. Usually, I was asleep before Mami came in. I wasn't afraid to sleep by myself with my portrait of Gabriel Valencia watching over me.

Whatever time she did come home, Mami always insisted on getting up in the morning, fixing breakfast for me, packing a lunch for school, and kissing me goodbye.

One morning, Mami wasn't in the kitchen. I looked into her bedroom, but she wasn't there either. I felt frightened and rang Tía Nicolasa's bell. Tía Nicolasa made me come in and eat breakfast with María Dolores and Manuel. She said maybe Mami had to work so late the night before, she simply decided to stay over at the restaurant and not come home. She told me to go to school and not to worry. But I could see Tía Nicolasa was upset and worried.

I worried. I couldn't concentrate on my work that morning. I messed up on my math test, and Ms. González told me to stop daydreaming and pay attention.

Just before lunch, Tía Nicolasa showed up, and María Dolores began squirming in her seat. She was afraid her mother was there for another parent/teacher conference, but I knew. I knew she was there for me. Tía Nicolasa was crying as she whispered something into Ms. González's ear. Then the trembling began. I could feel it spreading from my teeth to my shoulders and along my left arm. My fingers on my left hand, even the finger with my ring, began shaking.

"Oh, no! Oh, no!" Ms. González cried, backing away from Tía Nicolasa.

All of me was shaking now.

Ms. González looked straight at the class, straight at me.

"Gabriella, Gabriella, could you please come up here!"

Ms. González reached out to me as I approached her. She put an arm around my shoulder and led me outside into the hall. Tía Nicolasa followed. I could hear her crying.

"Gabriella, dear . . . I'm afraid . . ."

It was terrible. The shaking in my legs grew so strong I couldn't stand. Ms. González caught me in her arms, murmuring something I didn't want to hear.

"No!" I screamed. "No!"

"I'm afraid, Gabriella, we've had some terrible news."

Because I knew then, even before she said it. I knew. Maybe I knew all along, but it was too terrible, too unbelievable.

"Your mother . . . walking home so late at night . . . a drunk driver . . . your poor mother!"

THE NEXT DAY A POSTCARD ARRIVED FROM TIBET. IT showed high, snowy mountains. Papi said he really had a great outline for his book, and he would be traveling to places nobody else had ever written about before. He wasn't exactly sure where, but he would write again. He said he missed Mami and me very much and that he hoped to see us soon.

I put the postcard away and didn't show it to my class.

5.

SOON IS A TERRIBLE WORD. Grown-ups say it all the time, but kids understand that soon is never soon. Papi's *soon* stretched out for weeks, and then a month, and then two.

More postcards arrived, each from a different place. By the time I got them, Papi had moved on. Nobody seemed to know where.

"Don't worry," Tía Nicolasa said at first. "We will certainly catch up with him. It's only a matter of time."

"Soon," Tío Raúl said. "He will be coming home soon."

I STAYED WITH TÍA NICOLASA, BUT EVERY DAY I WOKE UP expecting to be in my own room, with Mami bustling around the kitchen, fixing me breakfast. Tía Nicolasa, for the first week after the funeral, spoke to me gently and never raised her voice. But suddenly, it was like every day again. The baby cried, María Dolores tried to get away with not doing her homework, Tía Nicolasa snapped and yelled at all of us.

"YOU HAVE TO HELP OUT, GABRIELLA," TÍA NICOLASA SAID. "You'll feel better if you keep busy."

"I'll never feel better," I cried. "And I want my father."

"I know. We're doing everything we can to find him. But that's the way it is with him. Anyway . . . one of these days he'll decide to show up, and in the meantime, while you're here with us, you need to pitch in and help out. You'll feel better."

I wanted to stay in our apartment by myself, but Tía Nicolasa wouldn't let me. I yelled and screamed and fell down on the ground and kicked my feet up and down.

"Stop it!" Tía Nicolasa shouted. "Stop it this second! You will stay here, and you will behave yourself, and you will stop having temper tantrums. Right now!"

So I stopped. I knew she meant it.

Tía Nicolasa's apartment was crowded. María Dolores and Manuel shared a tiny bedroom, while the baby slept in the same room with her parents. Tía Nicolasa said I could sleep on the couch. I didn't want to sleep on the couch, but she said I had to. No two ways about it! But she let me bring in my portrait of Gabriel Valencia and hang it up on the living room wall. She even took down a large colored photo of her own family in Mexico to make room for it. Tía Nicolasa had a lot of respect for the portrait.

"It's old," she said, "and ugly. Maybe it's even valuable. If you need to, you could probably sell it and get some money for it."

"I'd never sell it," I said to her. "Never! Never!"

NOW IT WAS SUMMER, AND STILL MY FATHER DIDN'T COME.

"He's never been away this long before," I told Tía Nicolasa. "Why can't they find him?"

"I don't understand it myself," she said, "unless he . . ."

"What?"

"Nothing. I didn't mean anything, but sometimes . . . well, sometimes he just doesn't seem to remember he has a family."

"Now, Nicolasa," Tío Raúl said, "leave it be. He is the child's father. Just leave it be."

"He's the best father in the world," I yelled. "My mother said he needed time to work on his book. She never complained. You don't know anything."

Tía Nicolasa narrowed her eyes at me, and then she

yelled, "You just watch your tongue, young lady. I'm warning you!"

TÍA NICOLASA PICKED ON ME ALL THE TIME NOW. SHE MADE me run errands—to the grocery store, the bakery, the laundry. She made me mail letters and buy the newspaper. Sometimes I had to go to the drugstore or pick up fruit at the produce market. She kept María Dolores helping at home. She said I wasn't much good at cleaning up around the house or taking care of the baby.

"My mother never made me run errands," I told her.

"Your mother spoiled you rotten. She spoiled the two of you. Your mother was a saint, but I'm not. So you just make up your mind that you'll have to pitch in like everybody else until your father decides to come home."

The days crawled. I waited for the nights. I waited for the time I could be alone on the couch and cry myself to sleep. My mother was dead. How could that be? How could it be that I would never see her again, never hear her voice or feel her arms around me? All my life, she had been there. I never even thought about it before, but now that she was dead, I remembered.

Sometimes I was angry, and I whispered angry words to her. I told her how I was suffering and blamed her for not looking where she was going when she crossed the street that night. I told her how Tía Nicolasa picked on me and what she had said about Papi. I told her it was all her fault. I cried and cried.

Then I slept, and my dreams were sweet. Sometimes in my dreams, somebody whispered comforting words to me in Spanish. Sometimes somebody touched my hair, and in my dreams, stood by the couch and watched over me.

Once I woke up in the dawn, reached out my hand, and almost felt another hand touching mine. I felt a warm glow, and I looked up at the boy in the painting and wondered if it was him. If he was coming to me as he had to Papi. If he was telling me to be brave and strong. It made me think more and more of Papi. He would come soon. I knew it now. Soon!

THE ONE GOOD THING ABOUT RUNNING ERRANDS FOR TÍA Nicolasa was that I could get out of the house and take my time about returning. More and more as the weeks passed, I thought about Papi. I thought about how happy I would be when he came home. I thought about how we would go away together—far away from Tía Nicolasa and her crowded apartment. And I began going more and more to Grandmother Russell's house. I stood across the street as I had with Mami and I watched.

I watched as the gardener changed the flowers in the

two large pots on either side of the front door. During
the winter, there had been red and white flowers. Now,
in the summer, the flowers were pink, yellow, and vio-
let. Another time, some men came to work on the roof,
and every day, at about four-thirty, a woman in a white
dress opened the door from the inside and left the
house. I began crossing the street so I could be in front
of the house at that time because then I could catch a
glimpse of the entrance hall when the door opened. I
couldn't see much, only a large colored rug on a dark,
shiny floor and farther back a big staircase.

My father had grown up in that house and could still
be living there if he hadn't married my mother. He had
picked love over riches like the hero in some of the stories I read. I wondered what it felt like to be rich and
live in a great house where you could afford a gardener
and a maid who worked all day until four-thirty.

I began walking up and down in front of the house
and daydreaming. One day my grandmother would
come out of the house, and she would see me. She
would recognize me immediately and hold out her arms
to me. She would beg me and my father to return to
her, she would order my aunt out of the house, she
would . . .

One day I arrived just in time to see the back of a
tall, thin woman with gray hair turning the key in the

lock and going inside. This could be my grandmother. My heart beat hard in my chest. I wanted to call out to her, but I couldn't. I watched as the door closed behind her. On another day, a face appeared at one of the downstairs windows but disappeared before I could get a real look at it.

.6.

ANOTHER WEEK, AND NO PAPI.
No cards either. Tía Nicolasa grumbled at night in the
kitchen to Tío Raúl when she thought I was sleeping.

"He's one great father," Tía Nicolasa said. "Promises,
promises, promises! That's all Estela ever got out of him.
What a selfish phony he is!"

"Shh! Shh!" Tío Raúl whispered. "I keep telling you
to stop. He is Gabriella's father, and you're upsetting
her."

"Well, she's going to have to wake up one of these
days, isn't she?" grumbled Tía Nicolasa.

JUST ABOUT EVERY DAY NOW, I WALKED UP AND DOWN IN
front of the big house and watched. If I came early
enough, before nine-thirty, I saw the maid in her white
dress arrive. When the weather was warm, they raised
the large windows downstairs but never opened the cur-

tains. The gardener came every week to trim the hedges and water the plants in the front and in the garden behind. I could see a piece of the garden from time to time whenever the door in the wall beside the house was opened. It was full of flowers and white wicker chairs. When my father was a boy, he had played in that garden and sat on those chairs.

There was a large garage under the house. Inside, I could see two cars. One was gray, the color of the house, and one day I saw the tall, thin woman with the gray hair drive off in it. It must have been my aunt because my grandmother would have known I was standing there and would have rushed toward me with her arms outstretched.

More and more I thought about my aunt. She was the one responsible for poisoning my grandmother's mind. She was the one who had driven my father away. She was the one who had refused to meet my mother or me. She hated me. But why? How could she hate me when she had never met me?

Sometimes the tears rolled down my face, and sometimes I just stopped and glared up at the house. I wanted to throw a rock through one of its windows. I wanted to stamp on all of those beautiful flowers. I wanted to go up to that big, fancy carved wooden door, knock on it, and say to my terrible aunt, "I am Gabriella Russell, named for Gabriel Valencia, and I hate you with all my heart. I despise you for making my wonderful Papi un-happy, and I will never, never forgive you as long as you live. If you were to offer me a million dollars, I would refuse. I would throw it down on the floor and stamp on it."

One day, as I was walking past the big house, the door suddenly opened, and the tall, gray-haired woman came quickly down the steps. "Little girl," she said. "Come here!"

I looked over my shoulder to see if she was talking to somebody else.

"No! I mean you!"

It was her—my aunt.

"Will you please come over here?"

I shook my head. What a cruel, mean face she had. But I would tell her. In a minute I would tell her. She moved down the steps toward me. "I just want to know why you've been walking up and down in front of my house for the past couple of weeks. What is it you want?"

I shook my head helplessly. This was real. It wasn't a daydream, and suddenly I couldn't speak.

"I've been watching you," she said. "Day after day, you've been walking up and down in front of my house. What is it you want? Do you understand what I'm say-ing? Do you speak English?"

The maid suddenly appeared, and my aunt, the gray-haired lady, said to her, "I don't think she speaks English, María. Will you ask her in Spanish what it is she wants and . . ."

María turned toward me and said in Spanish, "Now you just stop hanging around here. We've been watching you for days, and I'm going to call the police if I ever see you around here again. You just go on home now and tell them that we have a burglar alarm system in the house with a hidden camera, and if anybody even tries to come up these stairs . . ."

My fury exploded, and I could speak again. "I can speak English as well as you can," I shouted at my aunt. "Nobody's trying to rob you. I walk here because . . . because . . . it's a free country, and I can walk anywhere I like and you can't stop me."

Then the maid said, still in Spanish, "Shame on you to speak so disrespectfully to this lady. Don't you know she's going to call the police, and then you and your family will get in a lot of trouble. So you just go home right now, and . . ."

"No!" I screamed. "Don't speak Spanish to me. Let her hear what you're saying. I'm just as good as she is. I'm better because I don't make anybody feel bad and break their hearts."

"What's your name?" asked María, taking out a pad and pencil from her pocket.

"Gabriella," I shouted.

"I want your whole name and your address."

"Gabriella Russell," I roared.

They both looked at me in amazement. "Now you stop that," said the maid in Spanish. "You know very well that's the lady's last name."

"My name is Gabriella Russell." I began crying. "And my father's name is Philip Russell, and I'll never forgive you as long as I live for driving him away."

I didn't want to break down in front of my evil aunt, but I could no longer contain myself. I cried, and the tears rolled down my face.

"Now you stop that," said the maid, coming down the stairs. "And you go home this minute."

"I don't have a home," I howled. "My mother died, and my father doesn't know it. He's traveling, and I have to stay with Tía Nicolasa, who's mean to me and yells at me. I have no place to go, but one day my father will come home, and he'll get even with you."

The maid had reached me now and put a hand on my shoulder. "Now you go away this minute."

I put up my hand to push away the maid's hand. The tears were coming down my face so fast, I could hardly see. Nothing was happening the way it should have. Nothing was right. The maid gave me a little push, but then I heard a voice say, "That ring? Where did you get that ring?"

7.

EVERYTHING WAS NOISE AND confusion for a while.

I stood there sobbing while the maid scolded and my aunt asked questions I was crying too hard to answer.

Then they moved me up the steps, through the hall, and into a large living room. I was pushed into a seat while my aunt and the maid whispered to each other. The maid left, finally. She didn't want to. I heard her telling my aunt that she shouldn't be a fool.

I knew I should stop crying and hold up my chin and look them both in the eye, but the crying wouldn't stop. I sank my face in my hands and felt the tears oozing through my fingers.

It grew silent. The only sounds were my own sobs. I lifted my head and saw my aunt across the room, watching me.

"I'm not a thief," I yelled at her. "I wasn't going to rob you."

"No, no," she said nervously, putting out a hand toward me. "I didn't think you were. No, I just wondered . . ."

"She did. Your maid. She thought I was planning on robbing you. She said so. She . . ."

"Yes, well, she certainly was mistaken, wasn't she? I only meant to see if something was wrong. I had no idea . . . I didn't . . ." She stopped talking and just stood there looking at me. I dug in my pocket for a tissue, but I didn't have one so I had to wipe my wet face with my hands. It was humiliating. I knew I must look disgusting. I could see she thought so, too. So I pulled back my shoulders, held up my head, raised my chin, and looked her in the eye. I was a descendant of Gabriel Valencia, and I was just as good as she was.

The silence was terrible. My aunt cleared her throat several times, but nothing came out.

Gabriel Valencia! I held up my ring and said proudly, "My father gave me this ring. He told me it belonged to Gabriel Valencia and that it was given to the first child in every new generation."

My aunt nodded. "Yes," she said.

"I have his picture," I told her, "Gabriel Valencia's picture. I mean—now it's hanging in Tía Nicolasa's house.

I mean—she's not really my aunt, but when Mami—my mother—died—she was the only one around. I'm staying with her until my father returns. He doesn't know yet."

"Why didn't you contact him right away?" my aunt asked.

"Nobody knew where he was." I looked around the large, lovely room with its rugs and fine furniture. Over the white marble fireplace hung a painting of a beautiful woman in a white dress, holding a bouquet of yellow flowers. She was smiling very sweetly, and her hair and eyes were as dark as mine.

My aunt cleared her throat again but said nothing.

"Who is that beautiful lady in the painting?" I asked.

"Oh, that's Dolores Espinosa, my great-grandmother."

And my great-great-grandmother, I thought proudly, whose hair and eyes are like mine, and not like hers. My aunt's eyes were blue, and under her gray hair were strands of blonde.

She cleared her throat again, but this time she spoke.

"Where do you live?"

"Not far away—on Guerrero."

"I thought both of you—you and your mother—were in Mexico," said my aunt.

"I was never in Mexico," I said angrily. "My mother was born there, but she's . . . she's been here for most of her life. She never went back."

"I didn't know that." My aunt shook her head. "And I certainly did not know you both lived so close by, and that . . . and that your mother had died. When did it happen?"

"In May."

"In May? But it's nearly August now, and your father still doesn't know? This whole situation has been mishandled completely."

I began crying again. I didn't want to cry in front of this cold, heartless woman, but I couldn't help myself. "Nobody knows where he is," I gasped, "and I have to stay with Tía Nicolasa, who's mean to me and yells at me and makes me work for her."

My aunt slowly rose and moved over to the couch where I was sitting. She stood right in front of me, twisting her hands and murmuring something about "Now, now" and "There, there." Then she asked me what had happened to my mother.

I took a few deep breaths and told her.

"My mother was killed by a drunk driver. She was coming home from work at the El Toreador Restaurant. She had to work hard because we didn't have enough money." I said that angrily because I wanted her to know that it really was her fault that my poor mother had died. It was her fault because she was rich and lived in a grand house while my parents were poor.

"Oh dear," said my aunt, gingerly sitting down at a distance from me. "I'm so sorry. I had no idea."

The maid, María, came into the living room, and I jumped up. "Tell her to talk to me in English," I yelled. "I don't want her to talk to me in Spanish."

"I don't want to talk to you in any language," said the maid. "You certainly are a very rude girl."

"Well, you said I was a thief. You said . . ."

"Why don't we just forget all about that," said my aunt. "Would you like something to eat?"

I was hungry, but I said no.

"How old are you?"

"Eleven. I'll be twelve in December."

"She doesn't look at all like you," said María to my aunt. "And she certainly doesn't look anything like her father."

I asked eagerly, "You know my father?"

"Of course I know your father," María answered.

My aunt stood up. "María, I think I will take Gabriella back to her neighbor and . . ."

"Oh, no!" I jumped up. "What time is it? Tía Nicolasa will be furious with me. What time is it?"

"Ten after five."

"Oh, she'll have a fit," I moaned. "I was supposed to be back at four. Oh, she'll be furious."

"I'll explain the circumstances," said my aunt, "and then . . ."

"It won't make any difference. She's going to yell and carry on. She's always yelling at me—over nothing."

"Well, I don't think you'll have to worry about that anymore," said my aunt, "because from now on, you'll be staying here."

· 8 ·

"MAYBE I SHOULD GO WITH YOU,"
María said. She was looking at me suspiciously. I knew
she didn't trust me.

"Oh, no!" said my aunt. "I'm sure I won't have any
problems."

"I'll come," said María. "Maybe this neighbor . . .
maybe she doesn't speak English."

"She speaks English better than you do," I snapped,
amazed that I should be standing up for Tía Nicolasa. I
was amazed at everything suddenly. Amazed that I
should be standing inside this grand, beautiful house
and even more amazed that I should be standing there
with my evil aunt. But where was my grandmother?
Shouldn't she have rushed forward by this time and
clasped me in her arms?

"Where is my grandmother?" I demanded.

"Oh!" said María. "I was forgetting."

"That's right," said my aunt. "We both were. You'll have to stay in case she wakes up."

EVERYTHING INSIDE MY AUNT'S GRAY CAR WAS GRAY—AND spotless. The upholstery was gray, the dashboard was gray, and my aunt was gray. She didn't look at all like my father.

She cleared her throat. "Now there is one thing I must say," she said nervously, "and I hope you'll understand and . . ."

"You have to make a left turn here, uh . . ." I didn't know what to call her, so I just said "Uh."

She turned, slowed down a little, and continued. "I will need to see your birth certificate just to verify all this. I suppose you do have a birth certificate?"

"Everybody has a birth certificate," I said angrily. "Over there. Park over there."

She parked.

"That's my house," I said, pointing.

"Which one?" she asked. "That small house on the corner?"

"It's not so small," I said, although I knew that compared to her house, it was. "Six families live there."

"Well, well, why don't we go upstairs now, and . . . do you know where your birth certificate is?"

"I know where my birth certificate is," I said. "It's in a box with some papers, and a wedding picture of Mami and Papi, and some other pictures."

"Of . . . of you . . . and . . ."

"And my father," I almost shouted. I hated her—this cold, heartless woman—and I wished that I could say no, I wouldn't go back with her. No!

I hurried up the stairs, my aunt walking slowly behind me. The hall was dark, as it usually was, and I could smell the cooking and hear the sounds of people talking. I felt ashamed and I hated feeling ashamed. I could hear her clearing her throat behind me.

I didn't have to ring the bell. The door opened quickly, and a very angry Tía Nicolasa stood there, glaring at me. "Where have you been?" she snapped at me in Spanish. "I've been out of my mind, worrying about you. Oh!" she caught sight of my aunt behind me.

"Mrs. . . . Mrs. Serrano?" my aunt asked.

"What's going on here?" Tía Nicolasa asked in Spanish.

"I'd like to talk to you about Gabriella, Mrs. Serrano. Something very unusual happened, and . . ."

Tía Nicolasa reached out and pulled me into the apartment.

"Tía Nicolasa," I said in English, "I have to explain."

"What is it?" Tía Nicolasa demanded of my aunt in English. "What happened?"

She put her arm around me and pressed me hard against herself.

A few neighbors opened their doors.

"I think we need to talk privately, Mrs. Serrano," my aunt said. "May I come in?"

Tía Nicolasa nodded and opened the door. She led my aunt into the living room and motioned for her to sit down. She stood in front of her, an arm still firmly around me, waiting. María Dolores and Manuel came into the room and stood there staring at my aunt. She looked nervously around her, smiled awkwardly at Tía Nicolasa and the children. Then she saw Gabriel Valencia's picture and frowned.

"What is it? What happened?" Tía Nicolasa demanded again. Her fingers began patting my shoulder, and something moved from those fingers into my chest that made me take a deep breath and begin crying again.

"Oh!" My aunt refocused her gaze and resumed her awkward smile. "I think we'd better get this over as soon as possible. My name is Isabel Russell. I am—I think I am—Gabriella's aunt, her father's sister. Of course, I do need to see her birth certificate, but once I do, and we straighten out a few matters, I'll just take her off your hands."

THE BIRTH CERTIFICATE AND A PICTURE OF ME WITH MY father taken about a year ago convinced my aunt that I really was me.

"I suppose she may as well come home with me right now," said my aunt to Tía Nicolasa. "Of course, I'd like to reimburse you for all the time you've looked after her." My aunt opened her purse and pulled out a checkbook.

"No!" Tía Nicolasa said angrily. "I don't want any money from you, Miss Russell. She's like one of my own. I took care of her when her poor mother was alive. I've known her since she was a baby. . . ."

My aunt hesitated and looked around the small, crowded room. "I know it couldn't have been easy, and I'm sure Gabriella's father will want to make it up to you in some way when he finds out . . ."

"He doesn't have to make anything up to me," Tía Nicolasa said in a funny, cracked voice. "Gabriella's mother was my best friend. She was one in a million."

"Yes, I'm sure she was," my aunt said quickly. "And I know Gabriella must feel very grateful for everything you've done for her. As I've explained, my mother and I never realized . . . but . . . Gabriella, I think you should pack up some of your things now. You don't have to take everything. María will come back another day and get the rest."

"But what about all the furniture and the other things in our apartment?" I asked.

"The landlord is making a fuss about the rent," Tía Nicolasa added.

"I will get in touch with the landlord and pay the rent until my brother returns," said my aunt.

María Dolores and Manuel had stood silently in the room while the discussion was going on. Suddenly María Dolores began crying. "Don't go!" she said in Spanish.

"Be still!" said Tía Nicolasa in Spanish. Then she smiled at me and took my face in both of her hands. "Go, *niña*," Tía Nicolasa said, also in Spanish. "Your rich relatives will give you lots of things you can't have with us, and you'll be with your own family. That's even more important. But remember, Gabriella, if something goes wrong . . . well, it won't . . . but if it does, remember you can always come back. You will always have a home with us."

Aunt Isabel stood up. "I'll help you pack, Gabriella," she said. She rested her fingers lightly on my shoulder. "I think you should thank Mrs. Serrano for all her kindness. I'm sure you'll always be grateful."

G.

WHEN I REACHED UP TO TAKE down the portrait of Gabriel Valencia, my aunt said, "You don't need to take it now, Gabriella. We'll send for it another day."

"No, I have to take it now," I insisted.

"We have enough to carry," said my aunt firmly. "You can come back for it tomorrow or the next day."

I felt panic rising inside me. I stood there, twisting my ring and trying to think how I could make this cold, hateful woman understand that I needed my portrait so I could be brave and not scared.

Tía Nicolasa took my part. "It may be very valuable," she said. "And if Gabriella is no longer here, I wouldn't want the responsibility for it."

My aunt shook her head. "I doubt if it's very valuable,

but, of course, I won't insist if you don't want to keep it here."

WE EASED THE PAINTING INTO THE BACKSEAT OF THE CAR and put my other belongings into the trunk. My aunt repeated that María would return in a day or so and pick up the rest of my things.

Then, suddenly, there didn't seem anything further to say. We drove in silence back to the big house. My aunt parked the car in the garage and sat still in her seat. I sat still in mine, too.

My aunt turned toward me, pressed her lips together, and said, "Gabriella, there are many things we need to talk over. I'm sure you have questions, and I will try to answer all of them over the next few days. I have questions, too, that will need to be answered, but at the moment, I need to talk to you about your grandmother."

I watched my aunt's lips as they moved over her large, white teeth.

"Your grandmother, Gabriella, is a sick woman. She will need to be prepared for all this. I think it best if we wait until tomorrow to break it—I mean—to let her know what's happened."

My aunt's lips were thin and tight. They had no lipstick on them.

"I think we had better get you settled in quietly.

María stayed late today. She's getting your room ready, and I think we should eat our dinner upstairs in my room so your grandmother won't be disturbed."

I looked up from my aunt's tight mouth to her cold blue eyes. Papi's eyes were blue, too, but his were bright and friendly. My aunt didn't look anything like my father.

"Why didn't she hear us before?" I asked.

"She was sleeping then. She was in a deep sleep, and she didn't wake up. But sometimes at night she's restless, and I don't want to upset her, so I hope you'll cooperate and try to be as quiet as possible."

I nodded, but inside I was angry. Good! It was better feeling angry than scared.

THE ROOM MARÍA HAD PREPARED FOR ME WAS A LARGE bedroom with pink flowered wallpaper. It had its own bathroom and windows that looked out one side of the house.

"Was this my father's room?" I asked her.

From downstairs I could hear the sound of a high, thin voice and a lower one answering it.

"Of course it's not your father's room. It has pink wallpaper, doesn't it?" María said in Spanish.

I clenched my fists and snapped, "I told you not to talk to me in Spanish. Talk to me in English."

"Why not?" María asked. "You do speak Spanish, don't you?"

"Because . . . because . . ." I scowled at her and raised my eyebrows the way Papi always did.

María scowled back, but then suddenly she shook her head and said in English, "Oh, they're going to have a time with you; I can see that. But, considering who your father is . . ."

"Don't you dare say anything about my father! He's the best, the best father in the whole world."

María raised her eyes up toward the ceiling, but she smiled. "Okay, okay, let's leave it there. Anyway, if you want to see your father's room, I'll show it to you."

"You will?" I unclenched my fists.

"Come." María led me down a wide hall with a number of other rooms, all with closed doors.

"Now this one is your aunt's. She's right next to you if you need something. And this one used to be your grandmother's until she got sick. Now she's downstairs where she doesn't have to climb stairs, and this is another guest room, and here—here's your father's room."

She opened the door, and I looked into a big, wonderful room, filled with bright rugs, paintings, magazines, and a big bed with an intricate patchwork quilt. There was a fireplace with two comfortable sofas on either side. The wallpaper was a delicate blue-and-white stripe.

"Oh, it's so beautiful!" I said. "But . . ." and then I hesitated.

"But?" María asked.

"Well, it doesn't look like a kid's room."

"Of course it's not a kid's room," María said. "His mother kept redecorating it and redecorating it as he grew older. But this is the way he wanted it the last time."

Before he married Mami, I thought. This was his wonderful room. He gave it all up for Mami and for me.

We walked back through the hall to my room. Paintings of old-fashioned people hung on the walls. They are my ancestors, my family, I thought proudly. They are the descendants of Gabriel Valencia.

"My portrait," I told María. "I have to hang my portrait up in my room."

"Why?" María wanted to know. "What's so special about a funny-looking boy in a funny-looking old uniform?"

"He was a great man," I told her, "a great hero. He was a famous general, and everybody loved him. And he wasn't funny-looking, either."

"Look at that painting with the beautiful sunset you have hanging up here. And just look at that gold frame. I think it's the nicest painting in the whole house," María said. But she helped me take it down and hang the portrait in its place. As soon as it was up on the wall, I began to feel more comfortable. Now I would have my own room again, and every morning I would wake up to see Gabriel Valencia looking down at me. I would be safe.

But what would Papi say when he found out that I was living with my aunt in the house that was closed to him? Would he blame me? Would he have preferred me to remain with Tía Nicolasa until he returned?

No, no! Papi would never have wanted me to be picked on—although now it did not seem as if Tía Nicolasa had been as mean as I thought. Now it almost seemed as if Tía Nicolasa had really cared for me. It was bewildering, and yet, as I twisted the ring on my finger and looked up at Gabriel Valencia, I felt he at least must be pleased to be back with all his family.

WE ATE OUR DINNER IN MY AUNT'S ROOM. THE ROOM WAS cold and so was the food. Cold and plain—plain ham; plain baked potato; plain, limp, overcooked broccoli; and a plain green salad.

"María forgot to keep the dinner warm," said my aunt, "but in all the excitement, you can hardly blame her."

She ate steadily, but I poked at my food.

"I hope you're not a fussy eater," said my aunt, looking up. "I like plain food, and María is much too busy to cook anything elaborate."

We were eating on separate trays on small, separate tables. My aunt's room was as unlike my father's room as possible—a stark, severe room with a pale gray carpet, pale gray walls, a desk, a couple of hard chairs, and lots of books, but no paintings on the wall. There was only one beautiful thing in the room—a lovely white crocheted bedspread on the bed.

"Did you make that?" I asked.

"What?"

"The bedspread."

"Oh, that!" My aunt's face softened. "No, my grandmother made it. Not for me. For herself when she married. But she left it to me. She . . . I loved her a lot . . . she was very good to me."

"Was she the beautiful lady in the painting downstairs?"

"No. No. That was her mother-in-law." My aunt was still looking at the bedspread.

"Was she beautiful too—your grandmother, I mean?"

"Beautiful?" My aunt turned to look at me. "No!" she said stiffly. "She wasn't beautiful. Everybody said I looked just like her."

"Oh!" I said and pushed away the rest of my cold, tasteless food.

.10.

THE SOUNDS WERE DIFFERENT
during the night—a faint cry from downstairs; some
quick footsteps past my door; the wind hissing outside
my window; then long, strange periods of quiet. Before,
in the house where I had lived all my life, the sounds
never stopped. All day and all night, there had been a
continual jumble of sounds.

I awoke several times, unsure of where I was and
frightened, but each time, I felt something near my bed,
murmuring to me in Spanish.

I felt a warm glow and looked up at the portrait in
the dim light from the street. I didn't mind *him* speaking
to me in Spanish. I knew I was safe, and I fell back to
sleep.

WHEN I CAME DOWNSTAIRS THE NEXT MORNING, I COULD
hear people talking in the kitchen. My fingers slid over

the bannister of the wide staircase. How smooth it felt! The staircase in my old building had bumpy, paint-encrusted railings. My feet sank into the thick carpet on the steps. I stood at the bottom of the stairs, uncertain as to which way to move. The hall was large, much larger and darker than it had seemed yesterday.

My aunt suddenly appeared and seemed surprised to see me. "Oh, Gabriella!" she said. "There you are."

"What should I do?" I asked nervously. "Where should I go?"

My aunt cocked her head and inspected me. I had dressed in my prettiest flowered blouse and my red pants. "Is that the—uh—the best outfit you have?" she asked.

I looked down my front. "It's not my party dress, but it's the newest clothes I have. Mami—my mother bought them for me right before . . ."

"Yes, well, I suppose . . ." My aunt straightened up. "I suppose we'll have to go shopping one of these days, but in the meantime it will have to do."

"Is something wrong with me?" I asked, confused.

"No, no—you're just fine. Anyway, would you like some breakfast?"

"Yes." I was starving.

My aunt touched me lightly on my arm and turned me toward the back of the house. "Did you sleep well?"

"Y-e-s."

"Well, that's good." She led me into the kitchen, where María was drinking coffee at the kitchen table. Something that smelled like soup was cooking on the big stove behind her. "Gabriella's up, María. Why don't you find her something to eat while I talk to my mother."

María nodded and waited for Aunt Isabel to leave.

"What do you want to eat?" she asked, taking another sip of her coffee.

I looked hopefully over at the stove, thinking of Mami's hot breakfasts—eggs, bacon, and sausages . . . pancakes.

"There's cold cereal in the pantry," María said. "And you can toast some bread. They always have cartons of orange juice in the refrigerator."

"I'm hungry," I whimpered, feeling the tears begin to rise.

María seemed startled. She stood up. "I was forgetting you're only eleven," she said. "They never have much real food around, but I could make you some French toast. Would you like that?"

"Yes," I said.

I was still eating when my aunt returned.

"You're going to have to put some real food in the house," María told her. "Kids this age eat a lot."

My aunt sat down at the big table in the big kitchen and watched me eating. Suddenly, I didn't feel hungry anymore. I put down my fork, even though there still was a crispy piece of French toast, sprinkled with sugar and cinnamon, on my plate.

"You want some coffee, Ms. Russell?"

"Oh, yes—thank you, María."

María poured some coffee for my aunt, then poured herself some more coffee and sat down, too.

My aunt cleared her throat. "Gabriella," she said, "I think we have to decide . . ."

"Decide what?"

"Well . . . what you should call me."

I was embarrassed because I didn't know either. But I couldn't keep on saying "uh." I looked down at my plate and shrugged my shoulders.

"Would you like to call me Isabel? Would that be comfortable for you?"

"I don't think that's right," María said. "She's only a child, and it's not respectful for a child to call a grown-up by a first name. She should call you Aunt Isabel."

"Well—if she would prefer that. What do you think, Gabriella? Would you like to call me Aunt Isabel?"

I nodded but still kept my eyes down on my plate.

"Well, then, that's settled. Now—I've spoken to my mother—to Grandmother—and she wants to see you. What do you think, María? How does Gabriella look?"

"She needs a haircut," said María. "And I think she'd better call me Mrs. Sánchez."

"I don't think there's time for a haircut. Maybe later you can take her over to Robert's. And I've got to take her shopping for some clothes. I don't need to get her too many things until we know what her father decides to do. But until I hear from him . . ."

"Nobody knows where he is," I said, looking up.

"I have an address," said my aunt slowly. "It's a for-warding address, but I have written to your father and told him what's happened. Now, Gabriella, why don't you wash your hands and face and comb your hair. We'll go and introduce you to your grandmother."

. // .

MY GRANDMOTHER'S ROOM WAS
across the hall, opposite the kitchen. Aunt Isabel hesitated
outside the closed door and said in a low voice, "She's not
feeling very well today, but she is anxious to see you. Now,
Gabriella, just try to . . . try not to upset her."

"Why should I upset her?" I could feel the anger boil-
ing up inside me again.

"Shh! Try to keep your voice down, and don't complain about how Mrs. Serrano treated you and how you
couldn't get in touch with your father. And don't . . ."

"Isabel, is that you?" a high, weak voice called from
inside the room.

"Yes, Mother," my aunt said in a phony, cheerful
voice. "May we come in?"

"Of course you may come in."

My aunt gave me a warning look, opened the door,
and led me in.

The room smelled of medicine. It was a pretty room with pale yellow walls, a pale yellow carpet, and French doors that opened out to the garden. I sucked in my breath at the sight of the garden I had only glimpsed before. My eyes moved through those windows and over the green lawn to the brilliant flowers that bordered it. Would I be able to walk in the garden and smell its flowers? Would I be allowed to sit in the white wicker chairs on the terrace?

"Come here, child," said a voice from the bed. "Let me look at you."

My aunt's stiff fingers moved me toward the bed. I felt awkward and shy and kept my eyes down.

"Come closer, Gabriella. Isn't that your name, dear?" It was a weak voice but a sweet one. I took a breath and raised my eyes.

A beautiful old lady with snow-white hair was smiling at me from a bed draped with snow-white embroidered sheets. The old lady slowly held out a hand toward me. She looked exactly like the grandmother in my daydreams.

"Come closer so I can see you. Come!"

She looked so good and kind, I quickly moved forward. The old lady's hand tightened on mine and drew me closer.

Now it would happen. Now! She would put her arms around me. She would hold me close . . .

"You don't look anything like your father," said my grandmother. "Does she, Isabel?"

"No," said my aunt.

"My mother always said I had his forehead and his long fingers," I said quickly.

"I don't think so." Grandmother inspected my forehead and then looked down at my hand. "No." She sighed. "You don't look at all like him." She shook her head, and the smile began fading.

I had to force back the tears. Something had gone very wrong.

"My mother said . . ." My voice cracked.

"What, dear? What did your mother say?" My grandmother dropped my hand and leaned back against her pillows.

"My mother always said . . ." I tried again. ". . . that I was smart, like my father."

Grandmother moaned suddenly. "Isabel, the pain is really terrible. I need something . . ."

"Mother, try to put up with it a little longer."

"I can't, Isabel. I need to take another pill."

"Would you like me to read to you? Or would you like to watch TV?"

"No!" Grandmother pouted like a little girl. "I need a pill. I need a pill right this minute."

"Now, Mother, you know you're not supposed to take too many sedatives. You know they're addictive."

Grandmother's pout became an angry scowl. She turned to me. "You see how she treats me, my own daughter!" Her voice grew shrill. "She likes to see me suffer. It makes her happy when I'm in pain. Oh, my God! I just can't take any more of this."

"All right, Mother." Aunt Isabel's voice had grown cold and stiff again. "I'll give you another pill." She moved into the bathroom connected to the bedroom. I stood there helplessly watching my grandmother's beautiful, scowling face. Grandmother was looking angrily over my head as if I weren't there at all.

"Here you are, Mother." Aunt Isabel returned and handed her mother a pill and a glass of water. I watched as my grandmother's wrinkled throat gulped down the pill and then the water.

"Ah!" Grandmother leaned back against the pillow, and gradually her smile returned.

"We'll go now, Mother," said my aunt, "unless there's something else you want."

Grandmother waved her hand.

I felt my aunt's fingers rest on my shoulder. "Is there . . . is there anything else . . . you want to say to Gabriella, Mother?"

"Gabriella? Oh, yes," the old lady said. "Of course I do. Come here, child, and kiss your poor, sick old grandmother." She offered me her pink cheek, and I bent over it and kissed it. I smelled powder and medicine and something dry and old.

"Not so hard, dear," Grandmother said, kissing the

air on the side of my face. Up that close, I could see that Grandmother's eyelashes were covered with mascara and her wrinkled cheeks coated with rouge.

"Isn't it nice that you've come to stay," Grandmother said in a polite, faraway voice. "We will certainly have lots of time to get to know one another, won't we?"

The fingers pressed my shoulder.

"Uh—yes—we will," I said.

"Well, then, dear . . . another day . . . I hope I'll be feeling better." She smiled and nodded.

"I hope you'll be feeling better, too—uh—Grandmother."

"In the meantime, Isabel, I hope you're taking good care of Gabriella and making her lots of good things to eat." She chuckled. "Your dear father was always such a picky eater. When he was little, he would only eat tiny rib lamb chops and mashed potatoes with cream and baby peas." Her eyes closed. "I'm very tired now. Why don't you both go away, and . . ." Grandmother waved a limp hand, and quietly, my aunt turned me and moved the two of us out of her room.

"SHE'S A SAINT," MARÍA SAID LATER AS SHE WAS DRIVING me over to Robert's Beauty Salon for a haircut.

"You mean my grandmother?"

"No, I do not mean your grandmother," María said emphatically.

.12.

THE HOUSE WAS BIG AND UNFRIENDLY.

"Look around," my aunt said. "You can go anywhere you like. Just stay out of your grandmother's room and the garden."

I walked into the living room and sat on the edge of one of the sofas. I looked at the portrait of my great-great-grandmother over the marble fireplace. She had dark eyes and dark hair like me. She was beautiful. I touched my own face. Grandmother had said I didn't look anything like my father, but Mami always said I did.

I walked up the staircase, and my feet sank into the thick carpets. Mami would never walk here. Never. The big house was cold and unfriendly, like my aunt. She had poisoned my grandmother's mind against me. My grandmother was old and sick. I needed Mami. I needed Papi.

"When will my father get here?" I asked my aunt over and over as the days began to pass.

My aunt shook her head. "Now, Gabriella, you know I've sent him a telegram. Actually, I've sent two. But I only have a forwarding address, as I've told you many times. You must have patience. I'm sure you'll hear from him soon."

SOON? I DID HEAR SOON. AT THE END OF THAT FIRST WEEK Papi called.

"My poor, darling girl," he said over the phone. "Oh, my God! How you must have suffered. I can't bear thinking about it. And Estela! Oh . . . Estela!"

I began crying. "Oh, Papi, I've been so unhappy. So frightened. Please, Papi! Please! Come home!"

"I will, darling. I will. As soon as I can, but . . . but . . ."

"But what, Papi? What?"

"I'm in a hospital here in Japan. I was on my way home when I came down with some kind of fever. And then . . . hearing about . . . oh, Gabriella . . . what a nightmare!" His voice broke.

"Papi?" I said. "Papi?"

"I want to come right home," said my father. "I know you need me, but, Gabriella, I'm still very sick. I can't even get out of bed. But I'll come as soon as I can. We'll be together soon. Just be brave."

* * *

THAT NIGHT THE GHOST STOOD BY MY BED. I FELT THE
warm glow. I put out my hand, the one with the ring,
but I didn't feel his hand touching mine. "I'm trying to
be brave," I told him. "Just like you."

AUNT ISABEL SAID I NEEDED TO REGISTER FOR A NEW SCHOOL
in the fall—a private school.

"Why do I have to go to a new school?" I asked her.
"I liked my old school."

"Well, yes, I'm sure you did. Actually, I've contacted
your old school, and I'm glad to hear that you have a
very good record there."

"Ms. González said I was one of the smartest kids in
the class," I boasted.

"Well, the work is much easier in a public school,"
said my aunt. "But now that you'll be staying here—
at least for a while—we think you should go to
Harmony School for Girls. Your father agrees. I went
there, and so did your grandmother. And I used to teach
there. It's an outstanding school, and the students are
very bright."

She frowned and looked me up and down. "We have
an interview with the principal tomorrow, and today I
think we'd better go shopping and get you some suitable
clothes."

"What's wrong with my clothes?" I looked down my

front. Today I was wearing a bright yellow-and-orange tank top with orange shorts.

"Nothing," said my aunt quickly. "They're very—uh —colorful, but you'll need some special clothes for the interview—something simple. In any case, the girls wear a uniform at Harmony School, but we'll wait until you're admitted before we buy it."

The special clothes my aunt picked out for the interview included a white blouse, a pleated blue skirt, a dark blue cardigan, brown loafers, and white knee socks. When I looked at myself in the mirror the next morning before the interview, I saw a stranger looking back at me. The stranger had a short haircut, boring clothes, and a frightened look on her face. But when the stranger began twisting the gold ring on her finger, I recognized her. I raised my chin proudly the way Papi and Gabriel Valencia would have wanted me to.

"NOW JUST DON'T SAY TOO MUCH," SAID MY AUNT AS WE entered the grounds of Harmony School for Girls. "Let me do the talking."

Ms. Peterson, the principal, rose as we came into her office and smiled at Aunt Isabel.

"Isabel," she said, "it's been too long!" She came out from behind her desk and took Aunt Isabel's hand.

"Yes, it has been, Maggie. I've . . . I've missed you all."

"Well, you know, Isabel, we'll always have a place for you. Anytime you want to come back. Anytime!" The two women smiled and nodded at each other. They were both tall and thin with pale skin and gray/blonde hair. They didn't seem to notice me. I shuffled from one foot to the other, and Aunt Isabel turned toward me. "Oh! . . . and this is . . . this is my niece, Gabriella."

"Oh, yes. How do you do, Gabriella?" Ms. Peterson smiled and shook my hand. "Sit down, both of you. . . . Sit down."

We all sat down.

"Well, now," said Ms. Peterson, smiling again at Aunt Isabel. "I must say this is quite a surprise. A very pleasant surprise, of course. Because I never knew, Isabel, that your brother even had a daughter. How old are you, dear?"

"Eleven."

"What school did you go to?"

"Yerba Buena."

"It's a public school," said my aunt quickly. "I've talked to her former teacher, who said Gabriella was one of the best students in her class, and . . ."

"Well!" Ms. Peterson looked doubtfully at me. "Of course, we know what the standards in public schools are, so . . ."

". . . and she is prepared to work hard," my aunt said, "if she needs to catch up."

"We do have a very long waiting list of qualified students," Ms. Peterson said thoughtfully.

"In that case . . . ," Aunt Isabel said coldly and rose.

"Now, now, Isabel," said Ms. Peterson. "You know how we feel about families, and yours does go back. You and your mother were students here, and wasn't your grandmother also?"

"No," said Aunt Isabel. "She was raised in the East."

"Well, sit down, and let's see if we can work this out. Of course, we'll have to test her and maybe get some special tutoring. . . . But I'm sure she'll be happy here."

I wasn't sure at all. The two women continued speaking to each other as if I weren't there. Carefully, I looked around the room. It looked gray and unfriendly.

"As I told you, I used to teach here," Aunt Isabel said as we walked across the grounds. "I taught history to the older girls. I loved teaching."

I was looking over the empty schoolyard. School wouldn't begin for another month or so. Everything looked neat, and there was a smell of fresh paint from the newly painted school benches. Trees bordered the schoolyard, and on one side a garden with bright flowers bloomed.

"I also started the garden here. Look at those dahlias! I planted them with seeds my grandmother gave me.

She knew all about plants. Her parents had a farm. Just look at all those colors!"

My aunt hurried over to the garden, and I followed. "They haven't been weeding carefully." Aunt Isabel shook her head. "Maybe, if I can spare the time, since you'll be coming here, maybe I can come in from time to time and do a little gardening."

"I don't know if I'm going to like it here," I said nervously. I thought about my old schoolyard at Yerba Buena with its broken gates and scuffed benches. It wasn't clean and beautiful with bright flowers, but it was familiar. I knew lots of kids—even the ones who didn't like me. I knew them and they knew me. And the teachers liked me. Whenever I walked down the halls and met one of them, even one I'd had in the lower grades, they always knew who I was and said hello. I never thought about it before, but suddenly my old school seemed a very friendly place.

"Oh, you'll be fine here once you get used to it." My aunt knelt down and felt the soil. "It needs some fertilizer," she said. "I should have come around more often, but . . ."

"How come you don't teach here anymore?" I asked.

"Well, your grandmother became sick, and I had to go back home and take care of her. She had a nurse. She had quite a few nurses, but none of them ever worked out."

"Why can't María . . . I mean . . . Mrs. Sánchez take care of her?"

"Oh, she does when I'm out, but your grandmother feels better when your father or I am around. I suppose she's used to us."

"My father?" I said. "But he hasn't been around since . . . since he married my mother."

Aunt Isabel plucked some dying petals from a huge crimson dahlia. "Well, of course, he doesn't come as often as she'd like—as we'd both like—but whenever he's in the country he stays with us."

She turned and looked at me. "You mean you didn't know that he did?"

13.

AUNT ISABEL SAID THAT I
should keep my voice down when I spoke. She said loud
voices upset Grandmother.

I was very upset, but I tried. "No," I whispered. "It's
not true. We *knew* that you threw my father out after
he married. Mami and I *knew* you never let him come
back home again."

Aunt Isabel's lips tightened. She shook her head and
said, "I'll try again to explain, Gabriella, but I wish you
would listen and not keep interrupting as . . ."

"My father *told us* you disinherited him. He *told us*
you threw him out."

". . . as you're doing right now. And please keep your
voice down. I'll try to answer all your questions, but I
must say you're making it very difficult."

"You're the one who's making it difficult!" I shouted.
We were in Aunt Isabel's bedroom with the door closed.

"Shh! Shh!"

"I won't shh! shh! I won't," I howled. "You're lying. You're making it all up." I threw myself down on the ground and kicked my feet as hard as I could.

"Be quiet!" said my aunt. "You'll upset Grandmother."

So I stopped howling, but I kicked my feet up and down, up and down, silently, while my aunt just stood there watching me and waiting.

It's not easy having a temper tantrum and not yelling. After a while, I stopped. I felt foolish lying there, looking up at her looking down at me.

"Are you feeling better now?" she asked.

"No," I said. "I'm not feeling better." But I sat up and looked at her feet.

She handed me a tissue, and I blew my nose and kept looking at her feet.

"I hope, Gabriella," she said, "that we can try to be polite and reasonable with one another. I know we have a number of things to work out, but rudeness and insults never solve anything. Why don't you get up now, and let's talk."

I scowled, but I got up and sat down on the edge of her bed.

She kept standing. "Now I'm going to try to explain again, and this time, I hope you'll listen to what I'm saying. Let's start at the beginning. There was a time after your parents married when my mother was very upset. We don't have to go into all of that, but it is true that she and your father quarreled, and they didn't see each other for a few years."

"You didn't see him either," I said.

"Yes, that's true. I didn't see him either." My aunt raised her chin and looked straight at me. "You're too young to understand all of this, but your father—well, it wasn't well handled all around."

"It's because you and . . . and Grandmother wanted him to marry some society lady. You didn't want him to marry a Mexican girl. It was mostly your fault. You put Grandmother up to it."

"Is that what your father said?" Aunt Isabel asked in an icy voice.

"Yes—and that's what my mother said, too."

Aunt Isabel's face tightened, but she said slowly, "I've said it wasn't handled well all around, and I'm not going to say anything more right now. Let's go on. After a few years, your father and your grandmother made up, and he came home again whenever he wanted to."

"No! I don't believe it."

"Gabriella," said my aunt, "if you can't control your tongue, we'll just end this conversation right now."

She waited. I looked away angrily but didn't say anything.

"Your father stayed here whenever he was in the country," my aunt continued. "I realize now that he must have also stayed with you and your mother part of the time as well. I suppose—since it was a painful subject —he didn't talk about you to your grandmother. I'm not sure . . . but she seemed to think that you and your mother were both in Mexico. Certainly, that's what I thought."

"Didn't you ever want to see me?" I asked, close to tears. "Didn't you ever wonder what I was like?"

"Oh, Gabriella," said my aunt, "it wasn't like that at all. You just don't understand."

"I do so understand. You hated me, but you didn't even know me." The tears were now rolling down my face. "I'm sure my father—if he really did stay here— I'm sure my father told you about me. He loves me, and he's proud of me. I'm sure he never said we were in Mexico. You were the one who made it up. It must have been you. You were the one . . ."

Aunt Isabel stood up. "I think we'd better continue this another time," she said. "You're too upset, and so am I. Let's try again tomorrow. I'm sure you're exhausted. I know I am. Good night."

I CRIED MYSELF TO SLEEP THAT NIGHT. SUDDENLY, WHEN IT was still dark, I woke up. The ghost was there, standing near my bed. I put out my hand and tried to touch his, but I felt nothing. I looked up in the dim light at his dark portrait, and I whispered, "I'm trying, but it's hard to be brave with my father so far away. Aunt Isabel is so mean, and I'm so unhappy. What should I do? Tell me what to do."

Something touched my cheek, and I felt a warm glow. "I'll try," I said to him. "I'll try to be brave."

"I DIDN'T SLEEP VERY WELL LAST NIGHT," MY AUNT SAID AS we walked in the park the next day. "What you said really upset me, and I'm willing to admit that I should have asked my mother more questions about you and your mother."

I sniffed and looked around me at the people picnicking on the grass. My aunt and I had eaten a boring lunch at home and then driven to the park.

Aunt Isabel cleared her throat. "I think you also need to know that I wasn't living at home most of that time. I had to move back three years ago when your grandmother became really ill, but before that, I had my own place . . . and . . . my own life . . . and I was not that close to the situation."

"But you hated me. Why did you hate me?" I saw a man run after a little girl, grab her, pick her up, whirl her around, and kiss her. I missed my own father so much, it hurt me to see that man and his little daughter.

"I never hated you, Gabriella. I was busy with my own concerns then and just didn't think about anybody else. Now I realize I should have taken more of an interest in you and your mother. I'm sorry, very sorry . . . your poor mother . . . what a hard life she must have had!"

"No," I said, "she didn't have a hard life. She was happy. My father . . . she loved my father, and he was wonderful to her and to me."

My aunt was silent. I saw the little girl begin to run away again, laughing because she knew her father would run after her. She knew he would never let her really run away.

"I miss my father," I said. "I want him to get better and come home. I want to be with him all the time. He really loves me, and when he comes home, I won't be lonely anymore. I'll be happy."

"Yes," said Aunt Isabel. "I hope you will."

· 14 ·

I WROTE A LONG LETTER TO Papi. I told him to take care of himself and get better soon. I told him I missed him and to please hurry home.

Aunt Isabel didn't want me to go outside by myself. I told her over and over again that I'd been going pretty much anywhere I wanted for just about as long as I could remember. She said it wasn't safe and that I could only go out with her or María. Since both of them were so busy taking care of Grandmother, this meant I stayed in most of the time.

I began wandering all over the big, unfriendly house. The room I liked best was my father's. At first, I just stood near the door looking around at the beautiful room. I sniffed the air and could almost smell my father's after-shave lotion. Gradually I moved farther and farther into the room. One day I opened the closet door and looked at the rows of shirts, pants, and suits hanging there. They seemed new. I pulled out the drawers in a large, carved chest and found them filled with socks, underwear, and sweaters.

I had to admit that my aunt had not been lying about Papi's staying here. Why was it that my mother and I hadn't known that he had made up with his family? I kept wondering, and finally, I decided that he must have been worried about Grandmother. That was why he decided to come home and make up with her. Because she was sick. That had to be the reason. But my aunt said she didn't get sick until about three years ago. Maybe Grandmother had still refused to meet Mami and me, and he didn't want to upset us. But then Grandmother hadn't refused to meet me when my aunt brought me here. It was hard to understand everything. But I knew that when Papi came home, he would explain it all to me.

I liked to touch the beautiful, colorful spread on Papi's bed. It was a patchwork but made with satin and velvet pieces, stitched together with shiny silk threads. My fingers felt rough against their smooth surfaces.

I also liked to sit carefully on one of the cream-colored sofas and look through the magazines arranged on the coffee table in front of the fireplace. One of them was a travel magazine with an article written by my father. It was an old one, but I had never seen it before.

It was all about traveling in Spain. There were pictures of the different cities that the article described.

I liked to sit there in his room, looking at the article in the travel magazine and daydreaming about the future, when he could take me with him.

There was one wall full of photographs showing Papi with different people. Some of the pictures were autographed. There was a graduation photo of him as a young man, wearing a cap and gown. There was one of him as a little boy, smiling and sitting in the lap of a beautiful woman while an older girl stood next to them, frowning. I looked at the photographs over and over again, but I never found one of Mami or me.

EACH DAY WAS THE SAME. MARÍA ARRIVED EVERY MORNING except Sunday and helped Aunt Isabel take care of my grandmother. On Tuesdays and Fridays, a man named Newton came to vacuum the carpets, wash the floors, and clean the bathrooms. I didn't know whether Newton was his first or his last name. On Wednesdays, the gardener came to trim the hedges, weed, and water. Aunt Isabel liked to work in the garden when she had time and arrange big vases of flowers all over the house. I still wasn't allowed in the garden because Aunt Isabel said Grandmother was too sick and couldn't stand any kind of noise or sudden movements.

María cooked six days a week. She left enough food for us to eat on Sundays. She generally made breakfast for me unless she was busy with my grandmother.

"Tell me your mother's name again," she said to me one morning.

"Estela Russell."

"Did she used to work at El Niño?"

"Yes, but that was before I was born."

"Was she a little, slim woman? Very pretty, with big eyes?"

"Yes."

María smiled and nodded. "You know something funny? My cousin, Angie, was a friend of your mother's years ago. She said your mother was a fabulous cook. I met her a couple of times back then, and once she gave me her recipe for chile rellenos. I haven't made it in years, but people used to go crazy when I did."

"She made it all the time," I said. "My father liked it a lot."

"Maybe I'll make it tonight for your supper. Your grandmother certainly won't eat it, and I'm pretty sure your aunt won't either. They can eat some boiled chicken. Would you like that?"

"Yes!" I said. "Oh, yes! I'm so sick of eating the boring food Aunt Isabel eats every night."

"Well, she has a delicate stomach, poor thing," María said.

AUNT ISABEL TOOK A TASTE AND MADE A FACE. "WHAT IS this?"

"It's chile rellenos. My mother used to make it all the time," I said. "She made it better than this, but . . ." I put a huge portion of the delicious, spicy food into my mouth.

"It's . . . it's very hot." My aunt put down her fork and watched me gobbling my food. "I guess your mother was a pretty good cook if she was the assistant chef in a restaurant."

"She was a wonderful cook. She was better than the chef, but the boss didn't want to pay her as much because she was a woman."

"I'm glad to say that's changing," said my aunt. "Women have been discriminated against, especially . . . especially foreign women. But it's changing. Some of the best chefs in the city now are women."

My aunt picked up a small morsel of food on her fork. She looked at it and then put it carefully into her mouth. "It's . . . well . . . it's certainly interesting," she said.

AUNT ISABEL TOOK ME SHOPPING AGAIN AND BOUGHT clothes for me that were as plain as the food she liked.

She bought underwear and pajamas and socks. Everything was white or tan.

"I hate tan," I told her.

So she let me pick out a pair of pajamas with tiny pink flowers and a shirt with pale yellow stripes. She bought me my school uniform. It consisted of a white blouse, a dull green plaid skirt, and a dark green sweater with a small gold *H* set in a tan crest.

MOST DAYS, GRANDMOTHER WAS TOO SICK TO SEE ANYbody, my aunt said. I shouldn't take it personally if she didn't feel well enough to see me. As soon as she felt better, I could visit her again. I could hear her thin voice calling from time to time during the day, and either María or my aunt would hurry off to see what she wanted. I didn't believe my aunt. I was pretty sure she was purposely keeping me away from my grandmother.

"Does she ever get up?" I asked María.

"Not much anymore. Of course, when he's home, she does."

"When who's home?"

"Your father."

"I want to ask you something, María," I said carefully.

"Didn't I tell you to call me Mrs. Sánchez?"

"I want to ask you something, Mrs. Sánchez."

"So?"

"About my father."

"Ah."

"Did he . . . did he . . . ever say anything about me?"

María didn't answer.

"Did he?"

"Look, Gabriella, I just work here. I don't sit around and join in the conversations. Your father—he's here maybe once or twice a year. I don't see him that much, and I hardly ever talk to him."

"But did you ever hear him say anything about me?"

"No, I didn't, but I just told you . . ."

"What? You didn't tell me anything. Nobody tells me anything except her, and I don't believe her."

María muttered something in Spanish.

"What did you say?" I demanded.

María pointed a finger at me. "Go away, Gabriella," she said. "You're getting on my nerves."

.15.

I WAS SITTING ON THE STAIRCASE one day, looking up at the portraits, when my aunt came up the stairs.

"Oh, Gabriella, there you are," said my aunt. She always sounded surprised when she met me unexpectedly.

"Is that him? Is that Gabriel Valencia?" I asked, pointing to a picture of a man wearing a military uniform.

"No, no!" said my aunt. "That was his grandson, Rafael. He also served as an officer on the Presidio, but by that time, the Americans had taken it over. You see he's wearing an American uniform."

I studied the dark, scowling face. "He's so . . . so dark," I said.

My aunt laughed. "Well, his mother was Mexican, and his father was Native American."

"Gabriel Valencia was Spanish," I said. "Do you have a picture of him as a grown-up?"

"He was Mexican, Gabriella, and no, we don't have a picture of him as a grown-up."

"My father said he was Spanish, not Mexican."

"Well—Spain occupied Mexico at the time of his birth, but he was born in Mexico, became a Mexican citizen when they gained their independence, and served as a minor officer at the Presidio when Mexico took it over from Spain."

"My father said he was the *comandante*," I corrected her. "He was a great man who everybody loved. He chased away the pirates, and he helped the Indians. I want to be just like him when I grow up."

My aunt hesitated but then continued up the stairs without saying anything else.

EVERYTHING SPEEDED UP IN THE WEEK BEFORE SCHOOL started. First, I had to have checkups at the doctor and the dentist. Then I had to take a bunch of tests at school. In the past, I always thought I did well on tests. This time, it was different. Aunt Isabel wasn't happy when she got my results.

"At least," she told me, "you fulfill the language requirement. Of course, most of the girls at Harmony study French, starting in kindergarten. But Spanish is acceptable, and, naturally, you are fluent."

"How come you don't speak Spanish?" I asked.

"Well, I studied French in school and so did my mother. Your father, I'm sure, speaks Spanish, doesn't he?"

I didn't answer. I didn't know if he could speak Spanish or not. Mami and I always spoke English when he was around. And I remembered the way he always used to raise his eyebrows and smile at me when Mami and Tía Nicolasa spoke Spanish together.

"It does seem strange, doesn't it," said my aunt, "considering our ancestry. I suppose—let me see—probably the last person in our family who spoke Spanish would have been—Rafael Valencia's daughter, Dolores. She's the lovely lady in the portrait in the living room—my great-grandmother."

"My great-great-grandmother," I added.

My aunt seemed surprised. "Why, yes, that's true. She was your great-great-grandmother, and she was the last one to really speak Spanish until—until you."

"I don't speak it much anymore," I mumbled.

My aunt studied the other test results and frowned. "Your math is bad," she said, "and you'll need quite a bit of tutoring. Your reading scores are higher than average, but you will be up against girls who are highly literate. Hmm—your spelling is fair, but your grammar is poor."

"I was always one of the best in my class," I insisted.

"Well, Gabriella, I'm afraid that won't be the case any longer."

It wasn't.

My sixth-grade class was small—fifteen girls. All of them seemed to know one another. One of the girls was black, three were Asian, and most of the others had blonde hair and blue eyes. None of them looked like me.

I felt their eyes resting on me as the teacher, Ms. Baron, introduced me to the class.

"This is Gabriella Russell. Her aunt and her grand-mother both were students at Harmony. I'm sure you're going to help her feel right at home."

I could feel the eyes moving over my blouse, my skirt, my knee socks, and my shoes. My uniform, at least, was just like everybody else's. But then I felt their eyes settling on my hair, my eyes, and my skin. I sat down in the seat Ms. Baron assigned me near the front, and I felt the eyes resting on my back. I wanted to get up and run out of the room. But I sat still, clenched my teeth, and held up my chin.

The girls weren't really mean or stuck up.

A girl named Carolyn Tappan asked me to sit next to her in the lunchroom.

"Did you just move here from another place?"

"No . . . I . . . I always lived here."

"Where did you go to school then?"

"I . . . I went to Yerba Buena."

"Where's that?"

Another girl, Sarah Noble, said her older sister, Carolyn, used to have my Aunt Isabel for history. She said Carolyn told her that Aunt Isabel was a very interesting teacher even though she was a tough marker. Other girls spoke to me, too. I knew they had good manners and were trying to be polite. None of them spoke the way I did, and none of them looked like me. In my old school, most of the kids looked and spoke like me.

In class, they all sounded like the teacher. They read books I had never heard of, big books, grown-up books, and they used big words in the stories and book reports they wrote. Most of them raised their hands and knew answers to questions even before the teacher asked them. Sometimes I knew the answer, too, but I didn't raise my hand as I had in my old school.

I was no longer the best in the class.

A LETTER CAME FROM PAPI.

Dear Gabriella (it said),

Your letter reached me this morning, and I'm hurrying to answer it. I am getting better slowly, and hope to be home as soon as I possibly can. My poor darling! I know this is a terrible time for you, but I promise I'll make it all up to you as soon as we're together again.

I'm happy to hear you'll be going to Harmony School. It is one of the best schools in the country. I know you'll be happy there. Write me soon, and tell me how well you're doing. I'd be heartbroken if I didn't think you were happy.

All my love,

Papi

One day after school, when my aunt was busy with my grandmother and María was in the kitchen cooking, I sneaked out the front door, hurried across the street, and practically ran the rest of the way to my old house. I stood there as I caught my breath and looked up at it.

Inside the hall, the familiar murmur of sounds and voices wrapped around me. I was smiling as I hurried up the stairs and tapped at Tía Nicolasa's door. From inside I could hear somebody crying and somebody yelling. The yelling stopped, and I could hear footsteps approaching the other side of the door.

"Who is it?"

"It's me, Tía Nicolasa. Gabriella."

The door opened, and Tía Nicolasa stood there, holding the baby. "Gabriella?" she asked. "Is that really you?"

"Yes." I laughed happily. "Yes, it's me."

Tía Nicolasa looked around me. "Is anybody with you?"

"No! No! I'm all by myself."

Tía Nicolasa frowned. "Does your aunt know you're here?"

"No, but it's all right. Can I come in, Tía Nicolasa?"

"Of course, of course." She opened the door, smiling and nodding.

I looked all around the small, crowded living room. It looked wonderful. Tía Nicolasa had put back her family's picture in the place where Gabriel Valencia's portrait had hung.

"Sit down, Gabriella, sit down. Let me look at you."

I sat down.

Tía Nicolasa stood over me, smiling and shaking her head. "Just look at you—your mother would have been so proud. Just look at your uniform—like a real, rich little American girl. Just look!"

"But Tía Nicolasa," I whispered, "I don't like it there. I want to come back."

"Are they mean to you?" Tía Nicolasa asked angrily.

"No, not exactly. But I hate it there. I'm lonely, and my aunt's always busy, and my grandmother's sick all the time. I don't like the school. I want to go back to Yerba Buena."

"Do you get enough to eat? You look kind of thin."

"Oh, yes, but it's boring food. It's not what we like to eat."

"It's probably very healthy."

"I don't like it there, Tía Nicolasa. My father is getting

better, and he'll be home soon. Please let me stay here until he comes. Please!"

Tía Nicolasa shook her head. "You'll get used to it, *mi'ja*. It's for the best that you stay with them now. Just give it a chance."

"Please!" I sobbed. "I'll try harder, Tía Nicolasa. I really will. I'll run all the errands for you, and I'll come right back. I'll clean the house, and I won't talk back to you. I just want to come home. You said I could always come home."

"No!" Tía Nicolasa reached out and pulled me up. "You have a new home now, Gabriella, a new family. Go home now, and . . ." There were tears in Tía Nicolasa's eyes. "You belong to them now."

.16.

I HEARD SOMEBODY CRYING IN THE NIGHT. It woke me up. The cries became screams, and I heard quick footsteps hurrying down the stairs.

"No! No! I won't! I can't!"

"Calm down, Mother. Just calm down. Come on, now. Just get back to bed. That's right. . . ."

Then silence. A complete silence. A scary silence. I twisted my ring, and the ghost came. I felt the warm glow, and it wasn't scary anymore, and I fell back to sleep.

A NURSE CAME TO STAY. SHE SLEPT IN THE SMALL ROOM next to the kitchen.

"Try to be very quiet, Gabriella," my aunt said. "Your grandmother has taken a turn for the worse. I've sent for your father."

The news should have made me sad, but it didn't.

Now Papi would come home. Now Papi would have to come home.

"What's wrong with my grandmother?" I asked María.

María shrugged. "Who knows? She's been like this for a few years. Only when he comes home, she feels better."

"He'll come soon," I said cheerfully.

"We'll see," said María.

MORE AND MORE, AFTER SCHOOL, I WANDERED AROUND THE old house, studying the portraits on the walls. In some of them there were children, and often there was one child wearing the gold ring. I twisted it on my finger and wondered if those other children had also twisted it on their fingers.

Of course I loved my portrait of Gabriel Valencia best of all. But lately, it seemed as if the little boy's eyes no longer followed me around the room.

It was scary at night when I lay in my big bed in my big room and heard the cries from downstairs. But whenever I twisted my ring, the ghost came and stood near my bed. I could feel a warm glow, and I knew that soon Papi would be coming home. Soon! And then everything would be all right.

At school, Carolyn Tappan and Sara Noble often asked me to sit near them at lunch and play kickball with them during recess. Ms. Baron told me she felt I was making very good progress in my work and not to feel discouraged if I didn't always understand the math. People smiled a lot at school. The principal, Ms. Peterson, seemed to know everybody's name and often asked friendly questions about each girl's family.

"How is your grandmother, Gabriella? I'm very sorry to hear she's so ill."

"She's still sick, but my father's coming home from . . . from Japan, and she always feels better when he comes."

"Please give my best to your aunt. Tell her we're really thinking of her."

People were kind and thoughtful, but I could not get comfortable. In my old school, maybe some of the kids thought I showed off too much, but I had María Dolores for a friend. I always felt comfortable at Yerba Buena. I always felt like me. Here, even though the girls always invited me to join them, and I usually did, I had no real friends, and I never felt like me.

"YOUR FATHER CALLED TO SAY HE'LL BE WITH US AS SOON as possible," my aunt told me. Aunt Isabel and the nurse spent a lot of time in Grandmother's room now. Sometimes they left the door open, and I could hear my grandmother moaning and crying.

"I don't think you should stand there, Gabriella," my aunt said to me one day. "This isn't anything you need to hear."

"I want to help," I said.

"I wish you could," said my aunt. "I wish I could, too, but I'm afraid there's nothing anybody can do."

I spent a lot of time in my father's room, thinking about him and daydreaming about how happy both of us would be once we were together again. I straightened up the magazines on the coffee table and tried to put everything in order for him even though everything was already in order.

Sometimes María let me come along when she went food shopping. I liked to go with María and push the cart while she filled it. Most of the time, though, María shopped while I was in school and was busy cooking or cleaning up when I returned. But sometimes she was willing to answer questions.

"How long have you worked for them, María, I mean, Mrs. Sánchez?"

"Six years full time. Before that, they had somebody else full time, and I only came in when they gave parties."

"My aunt gave parties?"

"No. No. Your aunt didn't live here until about three years ago. Your grandmother gave the parties for your father whenever he was in town. I remember a big party about—let me see—seven, eight years ago. Your grandmother—she was still beautiful and healthy then —she wore a long white dress with red silk roses down one side."

"What did my aunt wear?" I asked.

"I told you before. She wasn't here."

THE HOUSE WAS VERY QUIET THAT AFTERNOON WHEN I came home from school. I looked into the kitchen for María, but María wasn't there. The door to Grandmother's room was open, and I stood there listening. I didn't hear anything. I looked inside, and through the large garden windows, I saw the fall flowers blazing in oranges, golds, and reds. Nobody lay in the bed. I hesitated. Then I moved slowly into the room and stood beside my grandmother's empty bed. It was neatly made up and snow white. The pillows were edged with lace, and so was the coverlet. I put my hand out and touched the silky material that made my fingers feel rough.

"Gabriella!"

I turned guiltily and saw my aunt in the doorway.

"I . . . I . . . just . . ."

My aunt moved toward me and laid a hand on my shoulder. "Gabriella," she said, "I'm sorry to have to tell you that your grandmother died this morning."

"But my father!" I cried. "He was going to come home and make her feel better."

"He's had a relapse, and his fever seems to have returned. I don't think he'll be back for the funeral. I don't think we'd better expect him."

17.

AFTER THE FUNERAL, AUNT ISABEL started having the whole house cleaned. The window washers stood on ladders outside the house and moved their brushes up and down each window until it gleamed. Newton came in every day with two other men, who washed and waxed all the floors. They took up the carpets and cleaned them and the floors underneath. They took down every lighting fixture and polished every part. They dusted all the paintings, and they even scrubbed the outside steps.

My grandmother's room was cleared out and all her clothes removed from the closet. Gradually, as the days passed and the windows remained open, it no longer smelled like a sickroom.

My aunt was very busy, directing the cleaners, answering mail, and sorting through papers.

"In a couple of weeks, the lawyer will read the will,"

María said. "Your father will manage to arrive for that, I'm sure."

"He had a relapse," I explained angrily. "He had to stay in the hospital."

"It's always something," María said. "He always manages not to be there when somebody needs him. But you can be sure of one thing. He'll be here for the reading of the will. Whenever there's money to be handed out, he always manages to be on time."

"That's not true," I yelled at her and stamped out of the kitchen. I ran up to my father's room, closed the door, and stretched out across his bed.

There was a question in my mind. I stood up and looked at my father's pictures hanging on the wall. Something in one of them puzzled me. I had to find out the answer.

I found it on a Saturday night, after María had left for the weekend. My aunt was in her room, and I tapped at the door.

"Come in!"

I opened the door and stood there. My aunt had a pile of papers in front of her on the desk.

"What is it, Gabriella?"

"I . . . I . . . wanted to ask you something, Aunt Isabel. Are you busy?"

"I'm always busy these days." My aunt sighed. "But come in. Sit down. I'm paying some bills and trying to answer a whole bunch of letters. I know this hasn't been a good time for you, and I'm sorry I've been so busy. What did you want to ask?"

There were a couple of empty suitcases on the floor and a pile of my aunt's clothes draped over a chair.

"Are you going away, Aunt Isabel?" I asked.

"Oh, not until your father comes, Gabriella." My aunt smiled. "Of course, I'll wait for him, but once he's here . . ."

"But what about me?" I demanded.

My aunt seemed surprised. "Well, your father will definitely be coming home soon, and once he's here, he'll be looking after you. Maybe he'll take you with him, or maybe he'll arrange something else for you. . . . There's no point in speculating. In any case, I know that's what you want, isn't it?"

"Well, yes, but where are you going?"

"I'm going to find my own place and resume my own life," my aunt said softly. "You know, Gabriella, I've had to take care of your grandmother these past three years, and my own life has been on hold. Now I'm just going to do what I want . . . even though I'm not exactly sure what that is." There was a sad sound to my aunt's voice.

"But"—she waved her hand—"what was it you wanted to ask me?"

"It's about that picture of my father, in his room. The

one where he's sitting on Grandmother's lap and you're standing next to them."

"Oh, yes! What did you want to know?"

"Well!" I twisted my ring on my finger and then held it out toward my aunt. "It's—he's wearing this ring."

"Yes?"

"But I thought it was given to the first child in every generation."

"Yes."

"Weren't you the first child in that generation? Why weren't you wearing the ring? You were about my age in that picture, weren't you?"

"I was twelve," said my aunt. "So I was a little older than you are now, and your father was four."

She stood up, walked over to her window, and stood there, turned away from me.

"But shouldn't it have been your ring?"

"Yes," said my aunt. "It should have been. It was."

"Didn't you want to keep it?"

"Yes," she said in a low voice, "I wanted to keep it."

"So why did you give it to him?"

My aunt was quiet.

I repeated, "Why did you give it to him?"

My aunt's back stiffened. "I didn't give it to him. She did."

"Who gave it to him?"

"She did, your grandmother. He made a fuss, and she made me give it to him. She promised me he would give it back, but he never did."

"But . . . but . . ."

"It was always that way." My aunt was still turned away from me. I couldn't see her face, but I could hear how she struggled to say each word. "I . . . I . . . couldn't do anything right, even though I tried . . . then . . . and now. It was never enough. She only loved him, and he . . . he . . . never loved anyone but himself."

"No," I yelled. "He loved Mami, and he loved me."

My aunt whirled around. Her face was pale and angry.

"No," she said, "he didn't love your poor mother. He used her, the way he used my mother—the way he used anybody who loved him. And you, too, Gabriella, be careful . . ."

"He loves me! He loves me!" I yelled at her.

"All that silliness he told you about Gabriel Valencia. All those lies about what a great man he was. Philip never grew up. He's always been a selfish, irresponsible child who makes up some kind of fantasy life about how great he is and how great even a monster like Gabriel Valencia was."

I jumped up and backed away. "I don't want to hear any more," I said.

My aunt moved quickly toward me and held me by my shoulders. "You're going to hear because you need to hear. Gabriel Valencia was a monster. He was a thief and a murderer and a smuggler. That's how he became rich and also because he cheated Native Americans out of their own land. His own children hated him and feared him. He beat them and brutalized them. His daughter eloped and married a Native American, and he murdered her husband—your great-great-great-great-grandfather. That's right, Gabriel Valencia ·murdered him. I'm sure your father never told you that. He was no hero, no great man, and nobody you should admire. Your father has never known the difference between what's real and what isn't. Listen to me, Gabriella . . ."

"No!" I yelled, breaking free. "I don't want to listen to you." I yanked my ring off my finger and threw it on the ground. "Here's your ring back. I don't want it anymore. I hate it, and I hate you."

"Listen, Gabriella . . ." said my aunt, sounding like herself again.

"I won't," I cried. I ran out of my aunt's room and into my own. I locked the door, threw myself down on my bed, and howled.

My aunt tapped on the door. "Gabriella! Gabriella!"

"Go away!" I screamed. "I hate you!" I pounded my bed with my fists and kicked my legs up and down.

"Open the door, Gabriella. I need to talk to you," my aunt said, jiggling the door.

"Go away!" I shrieked. "Go away!" I put my fingers in my ears and yelled louder than the jiggling of my door. I didn't stop until it stopped.

· 18 ·

GABRIEL VALENCIA'S GHOST CAME
in the night. This time it really was Gabriel Valencia's
ghost.

There was no warm glow. I felt cold and grew colder
as he approached my bed. He was whispering something
I couldn't understand.

"What? What?" I whimpered and tried to hide under
my blanket, but the ghost held out his hand, and I
couldn't move.

He came slowly, whispering all the time, and it grew
so cold that the hairs on every part of my body stood
up.

"No! No!" I screamed.

There was only a dim light in the room, but the ghost
burned with a hard, dirty green light. He wasn't a little
boy anymore but a horrible man. Everything about him
burned—his eyes and his teeth, his beard and his

sword, and his fingers, which reached out for me. I tried to twist my ring, but it wasn't there. Then I saw him pull the ring off his finger and hold it out—only it wasn't a ring anymore. It was a chain. It grew, and I felt it wrapping around me.

I screamed and screamed as he tightened the chain around my neck.

"Gabriella!"

"Gabriella!"

"Gabriella!"

I kept screaming even as the chain grew tighter and tighter.

"Open the door! Gabriella! Open the door!"

The chain was strangling me, and I cried out with my last breath, "Help! Help! Help!"

And then something else came and stood by my bed and touched my hair, and the chain fell off, and he was gone. There was a warm glow in the room, and I wasn't afraid anymore. I knew who it was.

"Mami," I whispered. "Mami, it's you."

"No," she whispered. "No. Ghosts aren't real. No . . . no . . ."

"No, no, Gabriella! Ghosts aren't real. You were having a nightmare. It was just a nightmare."

"No, there were ghosts. First he came . . . and then . . . Mami."

My aunt was sitting on my bed. All the lights were on in the room. I could see his portrait very clearly. I pulled the covers over my head and moaned.

"Gabriella!"

My aunt pulled the covers down and said gently, "I know you had a nightmare, dear, but it's all over now. It's all right now."

"I don't want his picture in my room. He tried to kill me, but then Mami came and she saved me."

"Shh! Shh! You're safe now," said my aunt. Then, very awkwardly, she gathered me up in her arms, murmuring something soothing, as Mami used to do. I laid my head on my aunt's thin shoulder and cried and cried until it was all wet.

Later, still lying in bed, I told her.

"It was him, Gabriel Valencia. He made a chain out of his ring, and he was choking me in it, but then Mami came and he disappeared when she came."

"I think it was a nightmare, dear. Really, I don't believe in ghosts."

"That's what Mami always said because she didn't want me to be afraid. Even now . . . even now . . . She said ghosts weren't real. And that's what you said, too."

"Well, never mind. It's all over, and you'll sleep now."

"Take his picture down, Aunt Isabel. I want you to throw his picture out. I want you to smash it up in little pieces and burn them."

"Of course, dear. Of course."

"It was so terrible. And I couldn't stop him. I tried to touch my ring, but it wasn't there."

"Well, Gabriella, speaking of the ring, I do think you should wear it again."

"I don't want it. I don't want anything of his, and besides, it's not mine. It's yours."

"No, dear, it really is yours now. The ring belongs to the first child in every new generation, so it would have come to you anyway. It's yours until a new child is born in the next generation."

"But it was his. And I hate him."

"It belonged to others as well. It was his daughter's, and her son's, and his daughter's . . . and it was mine. Here! Put it on. It belongs to you now." My aunt held the ring out to me.

As soon as I slipped the ring back on my finger, I suddenly felt safe again.

My aunt cleared her throat. "Gabriella," she said, "I'm very, very sorry. I . . . I . . . wasn't thinking when I told you about him."

"About my father?" I twisted the ring on my finger.

"Well . . . about him, too. I don't know what got into me. I suppose I'm still upset about Mother's death. But I never should have said what I did about Gabriel Valencia. I took away something that you cherished . . . that you believed in. It's not right—ever—to rob somebody of her dreams, even if . . ."

I leaned forward. "But how do you know so much about him? How can you be so sure?"

"I've read his own diaries and the diaries of his daughter and his grandson as well. And there are all the records the Spanish kept when they occupied the Presidio. They were great record keepers. I had them all translated for me. I've always been interested in history. You know that's what I taught at Harmony School, and before your grandmother got so sick, I was planning to write a book about Gabriel Valenica and . . ."

"No! No! Don't write a book about him."

". . . and other people in the family, too." My aunt smiled. "You know, Gabriella, he's not the only one you're descended from. You have many, many other ancestors as well as Gabriel Valencia."

"I don't know about them," I said, leaning back on my pillow. I wanted my aunt to go on talking even though I was feeling sleepy and my aunt's words were running together.

"Well, most people don't think about it, but we all have two parents and four grandparents. Now, when you start to multiply, you find that each of your grandparents had two parents, so four times two gives you eight great-grandparents. Multiply those eight by two, and that gives you sixteen great-great-grandparents. Now if you keep multiplying, by the time you get to Gabriel Valencia, your great-great-great-great-great-grandfather, you're talking about seven generations and —let me see—one hundred twenty-eight ancestors. You know, Gabriella, I've read somewhere that if each of us went back twelve generations, we'd all end up being related to everybody in the whole world." My aunt was really warming up to the subject now. I had never heard her speak so long and with so much enthusiasm about anything. She suddenly laughed out loud about something she had just said. I laughed, too, even though I hadn't really been listening. I tried to keep my eyes open, but they were slipping, slipping . . .

It was morning when I woke up. I was alone in my room with a space on the wall where his portrait had been. I hurried downstairs and found my aunt working in the garden. It was my first time in the garden, and I stood there shyly in the doorway watching her.

"Oh, Gabriella, there you are," she said when she saw me. She stood up and hurried toward me, as if I really was somebody she was glad to see. "Let's get you some breakfast, and maybe you can just take it easy today and tomorrow. Maybe you could even miss a day of school tomorrow. Would you like that?"

Later, for the first time, I sat outside in the lovely garden on one of the wicker chairs while my aunt weeded. It was a warm November day, and my aunt was wearing a broad straw hat to protect her pale skin from the sun.

"It's a beautiful garden," I said, looking around at the colorful fall flowers. "Did you plant everything?"

"Well, I had a lot of restoring to do when I came back home. The gardener pretty much took care of the bushes but didn't fuss with the flowers. Originally, it was my grandmother's." My aunt smiled. "Your great-grandmother, who laid out the garden pretty much as it is today. I have her plan. I'll show it to you if you're interested. Of course"—my aunt waved at a large tree on one side of the garden—"that redwood tree was a lot smaller, and all the fuschia died during the disease that hit them some years ago. But I'm trying to get them to grow again. I suppose there's probably no point since . . ." She stopped talking and looked sadly at me, but I was thinking of something else.

"How were you able to open the door to my room last night?" I asked. "I locked it."

"Oh, I have keys to all the rooms," my aunt said. "My mother kept them, and whenever . . . whenever she thought I got out of hand, she locked me in my room. I just used the key the other way around in your room last night."

"You mean you could have opened the door when I ran in and locked it?"

"Well, yes, but I realized that you wanted some time to be alone. It wouldn't have been right for me to intrude then. But later, when I heard you screaming, I knew you needed me so . . ."

But it was too embarrassing to talk about, and my aunt went back to weeding her flowers, and I turned my face up to the warm sun and shut my eyes.

19.

I SLEPT PEACEFULLY THAT NIGHT, and no ghosts came. In the morning, when I woke up, the whole house rang with the sounds of voices, thumpings, and bumpings.

María was in the kitchen washing down the woodwork and muttering under her breath.

"Where's my aunt?" I asked.

"Oh, she's here and there and everywhere. She's got Newton taking down the drapes in all the upstairs rooms, and she's waxing the furniture. You'd think there was going to be a wedding here instead of . . . and hey, you know today is Monday. How come you're still in your pajamas? Aren't you supposed to be going to school?"

"I'm not going."

"How come?"

"I'm . . . I'm . . . Aunt Isabel said I didn't have to go."

"Well, you can just go make breakfast for yourself then. She's making me wash down the walls and clean all the appliances. I thought we'd have a break after the old lady died, but no, she wants to have this place all spick-and-span for when the young prince arrives."

I knew María meant my father, but I didn't argue. The important thing was that he would really and truly be coming home soon.

I found Aunt Isabel in one of the guest rooms on the third floor. She was waxing an old table and was wearing blue jeans and a bandanna around her head. I had never seen my aunt in blue jeans.

"Oh, there you are, Gabriella," said my aunt, smiling. "I was just coming down to see if you were awake. How did you sleep?"

"Oh, fine."

"Well, that's good. I was thinking that maybe we can both play hooky a little later. I have so much to do, but we do have the rest of the week, and I have a woman coming from the agency tomorrow to help with the cleaning. Anyway, I thought maybe the two of us could take a picnic and go somewhere. Would you like that?"

"Oh, yes."

"Well, I just need to finish up in this room and the next. Tomorrow I'll try to organize all the junk up in the attic."

"Can I help, too?" I asked eagerly.

"You can today, but tomorrow you'll be going back to school," said my aunt.

"I don't want to go back."

"Now, Gabriella, you know you have to go to school, and . . ."

"No," I told her. "I don't want to go back to Harmony."

"But it's the best school in the city. I didn't know you didn't like it."

"Well, I don't. And I want to go back to Yerba Buena."

"But Gabriella . . ."

"No!" I said. "I won't go back to Harmony. I won't!" I clenched my fists.

My aunt narrowed her eyes, but then something crashed in the next room and we heard loud voices.

"Oh, they must have dropped one of those ugly mirrors," said my aunt, turning toward the door.

"I won't go," I repeated.

"Well!" My aunt shrugged her shoulders. "Your father will be home by the end of the week, and then we can all work it out together. Now why don't you go get dressed."

"WHERE ARE WE GOING?" I ASKED.

My aunt hesitated. "I would really like to take you to . . . to . . . but if you don't want to go . . ."

"Where?"

"Well, I thought I'd like to take you to the Presidio."
I looked down at my feet.

"If you don't want to go, we won't, but I thought we could just go over this one more time and then try to forget about it."

"That's where he was, wasn't it?"

"Yes, he served as a minor officer there in the eighteen-twenties, and his grandson, Rafael, also was stationed there in the eighteen-sixties. But, Gabriella, if you think it would upset you, we'll just go somewhere else."

"I'll go," I said.

"Good!" said my aunt. "I know a beautiful spot—I haven't been there in years—but I remember it. You can see a spectacular view of the bay. We'll have our picnic there."

IN THE PRESIDIO MUSEUM, MY AUNT STOOD IN FRONT OF the glass case containing a model of a Spanish soldier from the early nineteenth century.

"That's what Gabriel is wearing in the portrait," I said.

"His parents may have borrowed it, or most likely the painter loaned it to him just for the portrait," my aunt said. She paused a moment and then went on. "His parents weren't very good to him. His mother preferred his younger brothers, and his father beat him all the time. He hated his father."

"How do you know that?"

"It's what he said in his diary. He wasn't too good in school either, and in those days, if the schoolmaster had it in for you, he'd have you tied down to a bench and beaten. Gabriel Valencia was beaten a lot. I guess you might say he was an abused child. That was probably why he grew up to be a monster the way he did."

Later we wandered around the quadrangle.

"This is where Gabriel lived, but no houses remain from that period. The oldest building is the officers' club, which isn't really the way it looked then. It's been re-paired and remodeled many times since seventeen seventy-six. Now it's a restaurant and a meeting place."

I looked around me. Cars and people came and went in different parts of the quadrangle. Some laughing people were leaving the officers' club.

"It looks nice," I said.

"It wasn't nice then. It was terrible. The troops didn't get paid. Sometimes they didn't have enough to eat. Their adobe houses leaked, and every year during the storms, the roofs blew off. Children died all the time of disease. I think three of Gabriel's brothers died, and one of his sisters."

WE ATE OUR SANDWICHES UP ON A HILL ABOVE THE BAY. The grass was green, and down below, the sun shone on the bright sailboats and the sparkling blue water.

"It's pretty here," I said, biting into my sandwich.

"It's beautiful," said my aunt. "It's hard to think that the original settlers had such a miserable time and did such cruel things to the Native Americans who lived here."

"You mean the Spanish settlers and the Mexicans?"

"I mean all of them, including the Americans. We were the ones who chased the Native Americans off their own land, and killed them, and forced the survivors onto reservations. We still have a long way to go before we can shake off this terrible legacy from the past."

"I'm glad I live now," I said.

"So am I," said my aunt. "And the good thing about this beautiful Presidio is that now that it's become a national park, everybody is able to enjoy its beauty in peace."

"I wonder," I said. "I wonder if he . . . I mean . . . I wonder if people who lived here long ago had picnics, too."

"Oh, I think so," said my aunt. "I think people—even bad people—must have always had picnics."

·20·

THERE WERE MORE PICTURES UP in the attic. Some of them were stacked on top of one another; others were propped against the walls. Dust covered almost all of them—wedding pictures, family pictures, portraits of military men and of ladies in long dresses, photographs of children and old men with beards.

There were trunks and boxes filled with old clothing—faded dresses and hats trimmed with dried, crushed flowers. There were tiny satin shoes with high heels. Aunt Isabel smiled over a pale blue satin shoe that she held in the palm of her hand. "Styles in vanity change," she said. "Women used to prize little feet and tried to cram their feet into shoes that were far too small for them. You can just imagine what it did to their toes."

There was an old baby carriage made of cane and boxes and boxes of children's clothes and toys. I found a doll, a lovely doll, in one of the boxes. She had golden curls and big, beautiful blue eyes. She wore a pink satin ball gown and a gold crown on her head.

"Look, Aunt Isabel! Look at this beautiful doll. It doesn't look as if anybody ever even played with her."

Aunt Isabel looked up from a pile of books. "Oh— that! That's a doll my father gave me when I was— hmm—I guess about five."

"She's the most beautiful doll I ever saw in my whole life," I said, looking into the doll's face. I drew the doll close to me and brushed my cheek against her hair. It felt like real hair.

"He must have spent a fortune on it," said Aunt Isabel, picking up a book. "You can have it if you like."

"I'm too old for dolls," I protested. I tried to put the doll back in the box, but my hands wouldn't let go. "Can I really have her, Aunt Isabel? I mean, I won't play with her, but I'll just keep her in my room to look at. She's so gorgeous. What's her name?"

"I don't know." Aunt Isabel put down the book and picked up another one. "I never cared much for dolls. Oh, look at this!"

"What?" I was examining a tiny heart-shaped locket on a gold chain around the doll's neck.

"It's a book I loved when I was a child. I read it over and over again. It's still here—just about where I left it. I bet nobody's ever touched it since."

"The locket opens, Aunt Isabel, and look, there are pictures inside, tiny little pictures of a . . . a beautiful lady and, oh, a great-looking man."

Aunt Isabel was flipping through the pages. "Just look at this book, Gabriella. It has myths from ancient Greece and Rome. I loved those stories. Sometimes I used to make believe I lived back then." She stroked the book tenderly. "I used to come up here a lot when I was a child. When I was unhappy, this was my sanctuary. I'd spend hours reading books that nobody even remembered were up here."

I carried the doll over to my aunt.

"Who are the people in the locket, Aunt Isabel?"

Aunt Isabel was happily flipping through the pages of her book. "How could I forget? I haven't been up here in years. What did you say, Gabriella?"

"Who are these people?" I held out the doll with her opened locket, and my aunt bent over and looked.

"My mother and father," she said, turning back to her book.

"You never talk about your father," I said, "about my grandfather."

"There wasn't much to say," said my aunt.

"Why not?"

"He wasn't around much."

"But he gave you this beautiful doll."

"I never liked dolls," said my aunt. She looked up

into my puzzled face. "He never seemed very interested in me when I was a child. Your grandmother doted on him at first. They traveled a lot when I was little, and I always stayed with my grandmother. Her room was the one off the garden, where your grandmother died. It's a beautiful room. It used to be my favorite room in the whole house. Anyway, later my parents didn't travel much. They stayed home and fought, but I had my grandmother, so I could manage. They divorced shortly after your father was born, and I never saw your grandfather again. I didn't miss him, and I guess my mother didn't either. She had your father to dote on, and I . . . I had my grandmother until she died when I was about ten."

"I'll put the doll away," I said sadly. "I don't really want her anyway."

My aunt laughed. "It's all right, Gabriella. It's not the doll's fault. Maybe it's nobody's fault. Maybe it is. Maybe we just have to be grateful for the good things in our life and . . . and try to forget everything else. Anyway, isn't this a great place? I forgot how happy I used to be here. And, Gabriella, anything you find that you like, you can keep." She went back to the pile of books, making happy little sounds from time to time.

I carefully laid the doll down near the stairs so I wouldn't forget to take her when we left the attic. I wandered around, looking into boxes of other toys—a set of lead soldiers, some toy swords, and a wonderful Victorian doll's house with tiny crystal chandeliers and Persian carpets with fringes spread out on the floors.

"Whose doll's house was this, Aunt Isabel? Was it yours?"

"What? Oh . . . the doll's house. Isn't it beautiful? I did play with it because it had been my grandmother's. There's a box with some furniture." My aunt put down her book and stood up. "I'll help you look for it."

We found it under a pile of old newspapers. Inside were funny, old-fashioned pieces of doll-house furniture. There was a sofa with faded red upholstery. My aunt picked it up and said, "Look, Gabriella, isn't this stunning. Look at the carved wood frame. They just don't make doll-house furniture like this anymore."

At first it didn't look like anything but a faded, old-fashioned tiny sofa, but my aunt kept smiling over it and patting it. She took other things out of the box— little chests with drawers that opened and closed and chairs with torn woven seats. They all looked old and kind of used-up at first. She told me how she and her grandmother used to play with the house and how they made up stories about a wonderful family who lived there.

"Where is the family?" I asked her.

"Oh, there was no family. No dolls, I mean. We just made up stories about them. They were a very happy family."

She handed me a tiny mirror in a gold frame. It was speckled with old spots. "That used to hang over this oak chest. Wouldn't you love to have furniture like this?"

"Oh, sure!" I said politely. "Sure!" But then, all of a sudden, it did look beautiful, the way it must have looked to my aunt and my great-grandmother.

"I never saw a picture of her," I said.

My aunt was smoothing out something lacy. "These were the curtains that used to hang on the living-room windows. They're handmade, Gabriella, real handmade lace."

"Do you have a picture of her?"

"Of who, dear?"

"Of your grandmother, my great-grandmother?"

My aunt carefully put the doll's-house curtains back into the box and stood up. "All her pictures are downstairs in my room," she said. "We may as well go on down. We're not getting much done up here, anyway."

THE SMALLER PICTURES WERE IN MY AUNT'S DESK, AND THE large, framed ones were in her closet.

"Why aren't they hanging up on one of your walls?" I motioned to the empty walls in my aunt's room.

"Because they belong to me," said my aunt slowly. "I

took them with me when I left home. Mother didn't care. And I did have some of them hanging up in my own place. But when I had to come back, I never thought it would be for this long. I kept thinking she would get better, and then I could move again. I didn't think of this place as home anymore."

I studied my great-grandmother's picture. "She looks nice and she looks something like Grandmother, but . . ."

"But your grandmother was a beauty," said my aunt.

She took the picture and smiled at it. "No," she said, "I guess she wasn't a beauty, but she was such a good woman. You can just see it in her smile."

"What did her husband look like?"

"My grandfather? Your great-grandfather! Wait—here it is—their wedding picture."

I looked at the very handsome man in the photograph. He was wearing a tuxedo, and my great-grandmother was dressed in a fancy wedding dress that seemed to swallow her up.

"But . . . he's blond and blue-eyed just as she is," I said.

"Well, yes, he is."

"But isn't he Rafael's grandson? The dark man in a uniform in the portrait in the hall? He was even darker than me."

"They wanted to be Americans," my aunt said gently,

"and they wanted to look like what they thought Americans looked like. Rafael married a blonde, blue-eyed woman. His daughter, Dolores, the beautiful lady whose portrait is in the living room, also married a blond, blue-eyed man. Their son, Nicolas, was fair. So was my grandmother. So was your grandmother and so was her husband. You could say all of our original color was bred out of us until . . . until you came along."

"I guess I do look like my mother," I said.

"She must have been lovely," said my aunt.

"Would you like to see her picture?" I asked, embarrassed. "I know you saw her wedding picture when you came to my old house, but I have other pictures in my room if you're interested."

"Of course I'm interested," said my aunt, standing up. "Let's go look at them now."

·21·

THE WARM WEATHER HUNG ON
through November, and the flowers in the garden continued to bloom.

"I don't ever remember such a dry, warm autumn,"
Aunt Isabel said, kneeling beside a huge bush of copper-
colored chrysanthemums and carefully snipping off
some dead blossoms. "Usually by this time we've had
cold, rainy weather, and the flowers have begun dying."

I was busy cutting an assortment of white, yellow,
and wine-colored flowers. "What do you think, Aunt Isabel? Do you think I have enough? Do you think he'll
like them?"

"How can he help liking them?" My aunt smiled. She
broke off a branch of the copper-colored flowers and
handed it over to me. "Here, add this to your bouquet.
It's such a marvelous color."

I arranged the bouquet carefully in my father's room.

I had picked far too many flowers for the pretty cut-glass vase my aunt had given me. So I put the rest in my own room. My father and I would share the beauty of the flowers from our garden.

Today, finally, my father really and truly was coming home. We'd had a telegram telling us he would definitely arrive at four-thirty and that we should not bother meeting him at the airport.

"He'll take a taxi," said my aunt, "and be here in time for dinner."

Nothing remained to be cleaned in the house. Every cobweb and speck of dust had been brushed away. Every curtain and rug had been vacuumed or washed. All the mattresses had been aired and turned, the mirrors rubbed, and the floors and furniture waxed and polished.

"There's only the attic," said my aunt. "I can't cope with it. Maybe your father can."

My father! I thought about my father. I thought about how happy I would be when he came home, how exciting life always became during his visits. Now I would always be with him. Finally!

I went upstairs to dress at two o'clock. I wore my new party dress—a soft blue dress with small white flowers and a white lace collar. Robert had cut my hair again, and it curved around my face when I tossed my head. In the mirror, I saw a dark, thin girl with very large black eyes and a worried look, twisting a gold ring on her finger. I hoped my father would approve. He always liked me to be happy. I tried to smile and look happy. Even when I came downstairs to wait in the living room, I kept practicing my happy smile.

The whole house smelled of cooking. It also sounded of noisy kitchen sounds and some angry voices. María had hired two maids to help her prepare the dinner and serve, but that didn't make any difference.

"I thought since it's just a day or two after Thanksgiving, we might as well have a real Thanksgiving dinner," my aunt had said. "This is your first Thanksgiving here in the house, and we always had a big dinner in the old days when my grandmother was alive. I'm sure your father will enjoy it, too."

María was not enjoying it. "All this fuss for just the three of you—pies and cakes and ham and turkey and two kinds of stuffing and all those vegetable dishes . . ."

"Well, if there's anything left over, and you don't want it, we'll contribute it to Saint Anthony's. But if you like, I can give you a hand with the preparations."

"Please!" María told her. "The last thing I need is for you to give me a hand. Just stay out of my way, and don't waste my time talking."

All dressed up, I sat in the living room and waited for my father.

"But, Gabriella," my aunt said, "his plane won't be in

until four-thirty, and he probably won't get here until six. It's only two-thirty, and you're all dressed up already." My aunt looked me up and down. "You do look nice, dear, but you're going to be sitting here a long time before he comes. Don't you want to do something else?"

"Like what?"

"Well, you could read or watch television."

I shook my head.

"Or . . . oh, I know what. It's a little early, but why don't you help me set the table?"

I jumped up and followed her into the dining room. My aunt opened one of the chests and drew out a tablecloth embroidered with white flowers.

"My grandmother—your great-grandmother—embroidered this, too," she told me as we spread it out on the table. "She was a very fine needlewoman, as you can see, and this tablecloth was always used at Thanksgiving, so it's rather worn and stained. See—here—this faint round spot! This is where I dropped a dish of cranberry sauce, and here . . . this long, dark stain . . . your grandfather knocked over a decanter of wine because he was tipsy . . . and here . . . look at this mended part . . . your father pulled it and tore it when he was a baby, and . . ." Aunt Isabel went on and on, matching the stains and tears in the tablecloth with different members of our family.

We put white spiraled candles in heavy carved silver

candlesticks, and we arranged white chrysanthemums and ruby-colored dahlias in a silver bowl. We used fancy white china dishes with blue and gold flowers along the rims and placed clear crystal glasses behind them.

"I suppose this will be the last time," said my aunt.

"But why?" I wanted to know.

"Because I don't think any of us will be living here by next year."

By five o'clock, my aunt, dressed in a dark gray dress, had joined me in the living room. Even though it was a different room, and I was sitting there with my aunt, it reminded me of the many times my mother and I had sat, waiting for Papi.

"We could watch TV," my aunt suggested.

"There's nothing on."

"Well . . . how about cards?"

"Cards? I didn't know you played cards," I said.

My aunt shook her head. "There's a lot you don't know about me, Gabriella," she said. "And I suppose there's a lot I don't know about you. Anyway, yes, I can play cards, although I haven't for some time. I used to like—let me see—a game called fan tan and another one called honeymoon bridge."

"I don't know either one."

"Well, I'll teach you honeymoon bridge."

"I like to play poker."

"All right, you can teach me how to play poker."

We played poker for a while, and then Aunt Isabel taught me how to play honeymoon bridge. It was a much more complicated game than poker, and I had to concentrate.

"It's hard," I complained.

"I guess it is. It took me a while to learn it, too, but I used to play it with . . ."

"With your grandmother?" I said. "I bet it was your grandmother."

My aunt looked startled and then smiled. "I suppose I've been talking too much about her," she said. "I guess you're bored hearing about her."

"No, I'm not," I said, "because . . . because she sounds so nice, and she's part of my family, too."

María came into the living room. "I'm glad the two of you are having a good time," she said, "but it's nearly eight o'clock, and one of the girls wants to go home. She said she didn't expect to stay so long. I'd like to be home by nine also—but I'm used to working late around here. And by the way, the turkey is drying up, and the sweet potato casserole is burnt."

"I think, Gabriella," said my aunt, "perhaps we'd better start eating. Your father must have been delayed. He can catch up when he comes."

.22.

HE DIDN'T COME UNTIL AFTER
ten. And he didn't come alone. There were two women
and another man with him. I could hear them laughing
even before the door opened. I ran out of the living room
and stood there in the hall as Papi entered the house.

"Papi!"

"Gabriella!"

I rushed into his arms, and he hugged me tight and
spun me around. "Oh, my darling! My sweet girl! It's
been so long!"

He held me away from him finally and looked at me.
"And you're so big now—so grown. You look wonderful,
darling, just wonderful."

He pulled me against him.

"Papi! Papi!"

"Oh—Isabel—how are you, Isabel?"

I could feel my father's arms loosen, and I turned and

looked behind me. Aunt Isabel stood there, a stiff smile on her face.

"Good to see you, Philip. Welcome home!"

My father put one arm around me. With the other, he motioned to the people behind him. "I brought some friends home, Isabel. This is Rosie de Burgh, Petra Karnoff, and John Hurley."

The grown-ups nodded politely to each other.

Petra Karnoff stepped forward and smiled down at me. "Imagine you with such a big daughter, Philip. She doesn't look at all like you."

"No, she's the image of her poor mother," my father said, patting my shoulder. "She's a wonderful girl, and I love her with all my heart."

He bent down and kissed me again. "Oh, we have so much to talk about, don't we, darling?" I looked up into his handsome, smiling face and knew that everything would be all right now.

"Are you all better, Papi?" I asked.

"Yes, my darling, I'm fine now, but . . ."—turning to Aunt Isabel—"I'm starving—we all are. We've been talking nonstop since my plane arrived. I couldn't touch the garbage they serve on board, so I've had nothing to eat since . . ." He swung his arm around. ". . . Since . . . I've forgotten."

"There's plenty of food," said my aunt. "We were expecting you earlier, but . . ."

"You see, you see!" my father said, laughing toward his friends. "I told them I had to go home. I told them, but they insisted on meeting my plane, and they didn't stop talking for one second. It's all their fault."

"Gabriella and I have had dinner, and María has gone home," said my aunt, "but I'm sure I can scramble something together for all of you. Please come in and sit down." She motioned toward the dining room.

"Why don't we all pitch in," said Rosie de Burgh. She was a very beautiful lady with blonde hair and bracelets that jingled when she moved.

"Oh, no . . ." Aunt Isabel began.

"Please let us help," begged Petra Karnoff. "I know we're imposing, but Philip insisted we come."

"They may as well be useful as well as beautiful," my father said, laughing.

He kept an arm around me as he led his friends into the kitchen. Aunt Isabel bustled around, and the others followed along behind her, trying to be helpful. Aunt Isabel pulled food out of the refrigerator and began assembling dishes and silverware on a tray.

"Let's eat here in the kitchen," said my father, opening a bottle of wine. "Sit down, everybody, sit down." He turned, grinning at my aunt. "How about joining us for a late snack, Isabel?"

My aunt sat down slowly and said, "Thank you, Philip, but I've already eaten."

"That's right," said my father, "and you never indulge between or after meals, do you?"

"Not usually," said my aunt uncomfortably.

"Well, well!" Papi laughed. "Maybe Gabriella is hungry. Kids are always hungry. I always was. Still am. How about it, darling?"

"Sure, Papi," I said, sitting down next to him.

"Why does she call you Papi?" Rosie de Burgh asked.

"That's the Spanish word for father. My late wife was Spanish."

"Papi, she was Mexican," I said.

But Papi was busy pouring wine for his friends and didn't hear me.

They certainly were hungry.

"It's a good thing María made so much food," I whispered to my aunt, who sat quietly at the table, trying to look pleasant.

"This is really quite a house," said John Hurley, putting down a turkey wing and looking around the kitchen. "I'd love to see the rest of it."

"Later," said my father. He leaned back in his chair and patted his stomach. "Isabel," he asked, "is there any coffee?"

"I'll make some," said my aunt. "Do you want caffeinated coffee or decaf?"

My father laughed. "You know I want caffeinated

even though your poor stomach can't tolerate it. My sister," he explained to his friends, "has digestive problems. Her stomach gets upset very very easily."

Then he turned toward me and raised his eyebrows as he used to do when Mami and Tía Nicolasa spoke Spanish to each other. But this time I didn't smile and raise my eyebrows. I felt frightened, and I wanted all my father's friends to go home. I jumped up and said, "I'll help you, Aunt Isabel. I know where María keeps the electric pot."

"What will you do with the house now?" John Hurley asked.

"Sell it," said Papi. "Do you want to buy it?"

"Doesn't your sister live here?" John Hurley asked in a low voice.

"Not for long," said Aunt Isabel. "I expect to be leaving as soon as possible."

"Now, now, Isabel," said my father. "Nobody's going to throw you out. If you really wanted to stay . . ."

"Thank you!" said my aunt, sounding almost angry. "I do not."

". . . until I sell the house. It should take a while to get it in shape, and you're free to stay until then."

"I prefer not to," said my aunt coldly. "And I think you'll find that the house is already completely in shape—except for the attic. You can sell it whenever you like." She began measuring coffee into the pot.

"But doesn't the house belong to both of you?" Petra Karnoff asked.

My father smiled. "I don't think so. Of course, my mother's will hasn't been read yet, but I'm pretty sure she's left me the house. She loved it, but it really is a white elephant. I'll get rid of it as soon as I can, and then I'll finally have some real money."

His cheeks were flushed, and I could see that he was feeling happy. He turned toward my aunt and said in a friendly voice, "I should tell you, Isabel, that Petra, Rosie, and I have been talking about buying a winery in Burgundy. I'll try my hand at winemaking—in between my travels, of course, and . . ."

"And Gabriella?" asked my aunt quietly. "Where does she fit in?"

"Oh, Gabriella, my darling Gabriella," said my father, smiling and beckoning to me. Slowly I moved toward him, and he pulled me over to him and began smoothing my hair. "Of course, she'll come with me to France. I'll find a good boarding school for her. I'll have enough money now to send her to one of the best. Nothing will be too good for my baby."

I put my arms around Papi's neck and whispered in his ear. "Please, Papi, I don't want to go to a French school. I can't speak French."

"Oh, you'll learn French in school, Gabriella. They'll make a little French girl out of you. And you'll see me lots. We'll go skiing together, and when you get a little bigger, you can come with me on some of my trips."

"But Papi, I'm scared. I . . . I think I want to stay here."

My father brushed my hair back from my forehead and kissed my head. "You'll be happy there, darling. You'll make friends, and I really will try to see you as much as possible." He looked at my worried face and pushed my chin up. "Now you know I like to see happy faces. Come on, Gabriella. Let me see a happy face."

I tried. I really did. I raised my chin and I tried to shape my lips into a smile. I could hear the clatter of plates and the clink of glasses. I could hear my father's voice, and I suddenly felt as if I were going to burst.

"No!" I screamed. "No! I won't! I won't! I won't!"

I dropped down on the ground, kicking my legs and screaming as loud as I could. But not so loud that I couldn't hear my father say, "What's wrong, Gabriella? What's wrong? What in the world's got into her?"

And then somebody picked me up and held me so tight it hurt. I put my arms around her neck and I knew that I didn't want anybody, not even him, to take me away from her.

23.

MY FATHER HAD TEARS IN HIS EYES.

"All those months in the hospital," he said, "I thought about you . . . about how we'd finally be together when I got well. I thought about how I'd make it up to you. I couldn't wait to see you."

"But you brought them home with you last night—those people. If you couldn't wait to see me, how come you didn't come right home from the airport? And how come you brought them home with you?"

"Gabriella, Gabriella," said my father, reaching out and taking my hand. We were sitting together the next day on one of the cream-colored sofas in his beautiful room with the bouquet of flowers I had picked for him on the coffee table in front of us.

I let him take my hand, but I didn't return the pressure of his. "Gabriella, they were old, old friends. They insisted on meeting my plane. We've been friends for years."

"If you've been friends for years," I said, "how come you never brought them home? Mami always asked you to bring your friends home, but you never did. How come?" I pulled my hand away from his.

"Oh, Gabriella, your poor mother. Oh, I can't bear it!"

He put his face into his hands. I moved farther away from him.

"And how come," I said, "how come you never told Grandmother about us? How come?"

He raised his face. It was covered with tears. I looked away, at the bouquet. One of the copper flowers drooped and hung awkwardly on its stem.

"I tried, Gabriella, many, many times. But she was a sick woman, and your aunt didn't help."

"No!" I said. "No! You always blamed Aunt Isabel, but I know now that's not so. She didn't even live here until three years ago. You never tried to tell Grandmother. You were ashamed of us, ashamed of Mami and . . . and me. Grandmother gave you money, I know, but you never gave us any. Mami had to work twice as hard while you traveled all over the world enjoying yourself. And you couldn't even make it back when Grandmother was dying. María told me that's the way it always was, but that you would always be sure to come back when money was involved."

"Oh, that's what María said, was it? Well, I'll say a few words to María, you can be sure of that. But Gabriella, believe me, Gabriella, I was planning to tell your grandmother after I came back from this trip."

"I don't believe you," I told him. "You're always lying. You told me all those lies about Gabriel Valencia. I believed you, but it wasn't true."

"It was true," said my father. "He was a great man, the *comandante* of the Presidio, a brave, kind man . . ."

"He was a monster—a cruel, evil man. He killed lots of people, and he killed my great-great-great-great-grandfather because he was Native American. He was ashamed of him just the way you were ashamed of Mami and me."

"I can guess who told you all that, but, Gabriella . . ."

"And you named me after him, and you told me his ghost came and gave you courage."

"Yes, he did."

"Well, he came to me, and he tried to strangle me in a chain. But then Mami came and stopped him. Aunt Isabel said it was only a nightmare, but I know it wasn't."

"You're upset, my poor darling," said my father, "and no wonder, considering what you've been through. But I'll make it up to you. You'll see."

"No," I said, standing up. "I don't believe you anymore, and I don't want to go with you. I want to stay here with Aunt Isabel."

"Aunt Isabel?" laughed my father, raising his eyebrows. "I doubt if she wants to be stuck with you."

I wasn't sure either. I waited to hear what she would say when my father spoke to her about it. But there seemed to be some unfinished business he had with María before he would even talk to my aunt. He wanted to fire María.

"It isn't up to you," said my aunt, "to fire María."

"Yes, it is," said my father. "She badmouths me to everybody, and I'm not going to stand for it anymore. She has no respect for me. Never did. This is my house now, and I say she's fired as of this minute."

"This is not your house until after the will is read, and until then," said my aunt firmly, "María stays."

"I say María goes."

"I say you call me Mrs. Sánchez," María said to my father.

"You should be ashamed," my aunt said coldly to my father. "To have so little respect for somebody who took care of your sick mother and helped me look after your neglected child. From now on you call María Mrs. Sánchez."

"And you, too, Ms. Russell," María said. "I want you to call me Mrs. Sánchez, too. I like you a lot, Ms. Russell.

I think you're a real saint, but from now on, I want everybody to call me Mrs. Sánchez."

"Oh!" said my aunt.

I HAD TO WAIT UNTIL THE NEXT DAY BEFORE THEY GOT around to me.

"And you've been filling her head with all sorts of lies and nonsense," my father said to my aunt.

Both of them were in the living room. I was sitting on the stairs, listening. I'd been spending a lot of time listening for what I hoped I would hear.

"Who's been filling her head with lies and nonsense?" snapped my aunt. "Who let her live in poverty all these years while he was traveling in comfort all over the world? Who didn't care what happened to her after her poor mother died? If it weren't for Mrs. Serrano, that kind neighbor of hers . . ."

"She turned Gabriella against me, too," said my father. "You all did. But once I get her away from all of you, she'll be herself again."

"I won't let you take her away from me," said my aunt. "I'll fight you in every court in the land. I'll hide her from you. I'll bring witnesses to say how you neglected her and neglected her mother. I love her, and I want her to be with me."

And that's what I was waiting to hear. "I want to be

with you, too," I shouted, bursting into the room and burying my head in my aunt's lap. "Make him go away, Aunt Isabel. Make him go away now."

THE WILL WAS READ A FEW DAYS LATER. MY FATHER, AS he had expected, inherited the house and the bulk of Grandmother's fortune. My aunt was left with a small trust fund, some jewelry, and any pieces of furniture in the house she wanted.

"We'll start packing right away, Gabriella," she said after we returned home from the lawyer's office. "The sooner we get out of here, the better."

"But where will we go? And what will Papi—no— I'm never going to call him that again—what will my father do about me?"

My aunt waved her hand impatiently. "He won't do anything, just like he never did. Don't worry, Gabriella. You're coming with me."

"Where will we go, Aunt Isabel?"

Mrs. Sánchez came into my aunt's room, a grim look on her face. "I'm quitting, Ms. Russell," she said. "Right now!"

"Oh," said my aunt unhappily, "I was hoping you could stay a few days and help Gabriella and me."

"He wants me to cook a big dinner tomorrow night."

"I thought he wasn't talking to you."

"Well, now he is. He wants me to cook a big dinner for him and about twenty of his friends. So I'm quitting right now."

"Oh, María!"

"Now, Ms. Russell, you know I asked you to call me Mrs. Sánchez."

"No," said my aunt, looking at her shyly, "I really don't want to do that. But . . . but if it's all right with you, maybe you could call me Isabel."

María looked at my aunt, nodded, and smiled. "Okay, Isabel, I'm quitting."

"Oh, Lord!" said my aunt.

"But I'll help you out as a friend. I won't lift a finger for him, but I will for you."

MY FATHER SPOKE TO ME ONE LAST TIME BEFORE WE LEFT.

"I have to be away for a few days," he said, "but I'll be back before you move out. At any rate, I've decided that it probably would be best if you stayed here in San Francisco. Your Aunt Isabel will be your guardian as long as I think that's best for you. Do you understand, Gabriella?"

"No," I said. "I don't understand. I want to stay with Aunt Isabel, and she wants me to stay with her. That's all I understand."

"You know, Gabriella," said my father, "I only want

the best for you. That's all I've ever wanted. I want you to be happy, and if you want to stay here with your aunt and go to Harmony School . . ."

"No," I said. "I won't go to Harmony School. I'm going to public school."

"Did your aunt put you up to this?"

"No. She wants me to go to Harmony School, too, but I won't! I won't!"

"Now, you just calm down, Gabriella! Calm down! I don't want to see another temper tantrum like I did the other night. You disgraced me in front of my friends."

"Can I go now?" I asked.

My father put up his hand. "You and your aunt will have to work out some of these problems yourselves," he said. "But Gabriella . . . Gabriella, darling . . . I want you to know I love you and that I'll always be there for you if you need me. I will be sending your aunt some money for you—there will be plenty, so you'll always have enough. And you can write me if you need anything or would like to spend some time with me . . ."

He leaned over, ruffled my hair, and tried to kiss me, but I pulled away.

"Can I go now?" I said.

"Gabriella." There were tears in his eyes. "You probably think I haven't been a very good father . . ."

I moved toward the door.

"But I love you very much, and I loved Mami. Please, Gabriella, believe me. Please, don't forget me."

I opened the door and looked back at him. "No," I said, "I won't forget you." Then I went out of his room and closed the door.

24.

MY AUNT GATHERED SEEDS AND cuttings from the garden. She packed some of the portraits, a few pieces of furniture, her grandmother's tablecloth, and her bedspread. I took the doll, the doll's house with its furniture, some of the old-fashioned dresses I found up in the attic, and the book of Greek and Roman myths.

"I managed to find an apartment in the building I used to live in," Aunt Isabel said. "It's not too big, but it does have a nice yard, so I'll be able to plant my seeds. As I've told you, I also plan to teach again at Harmony School," she added, narrowing her eyes at me.

"I won't," I said, clenching my fists. "I won't go there. I want to go to public school. I will go to public school. I want to be me."

"But why? Just tell me why. Harmony is a much better school."

"Who cares?"

"Was somebody mean to you at Harmony? Did somebody insult you?"

"No."

"So why would you prefer to go to an inferior school where you won't learn as much?" She sounded exasperated.

"I'll study harder," I said, and then I tried to explain. "I don't want . . . I don't want . . . what I am . . . to be bred out of me the way you said Gabriel Valencia's descendants bred their original color out of themselves. I don't want to feel I'm not as good as . . . as anybody else. I don't want anybody . . . to raise his or her eyebrows at me because I'm me. I'm somebody with dark hair and dark skin, and I speak Spanish. I don't want to feel bad because I'm me."

"But that's ridiculous, Gabriella. Nowadays we all believe that everybody is just as good as anybody else whatever he or she looks like."

My aunt didn't understand. I loved her a lot, but I knew there were some things about me she would never understand. But I also knew she would try.

"I'm going to public school," I said. "I won't go to Harmony. I just won't!"

My aunt sighed. "It's not going to be easy living with you, but then again, I guess it won't be easy for you living with me. Why don't we talk about this another time?"

But I had something else on my mind. "What did you do with the portrait?" I asked. "Did you throw it out like I asked you to?"

My aunt narrowed her eyes again. "No, I did not, Gabriella. I didn't think it was up to you or to me to dispose of a real piece of history. Your father says he doesn't want it, so I'm planning to give it to the Presidio Museum, along with most of the other portraits."

"Is it here? Now?"

"Well, yes, it is. Down in the basement. Covered up."

"Can I see it?"

"Do you think you should? I'm not sure that's such a good idea."

"Will you come with me?"

I HAD NEVER BEEN DOWN TO THE BASEMENT BEFORE. IT WAS gloomy, filled with dusty pieces of furniture and stacks of boxes. It smelled old and damp.

"It smells bad here," I said.

"Well, it is a very old house and it smells like one."

"How old is it?"

"Over a hundred years old. Rafael, Gabriel's grandson, had it built in eighteen eighty-seven, just a few years before he died." She hesitated. "He wasn't a very nice man either, but he was probably the one person Gabriel really loved."

"Where's the portrait?"

"Back here—behind this old chest." Aunt Isabel pulled on a chain that hung from a naked bulb, and a dim light came on. "Are you sure you want to see it?"

"Yes."

My aunt moved the portrait out from behind the chest. It was covered with an old cloth. She pulled the cloth off, came over to where I was standing, and took my hand.

I looked at the boy in the painting. I had been looking at him for most of my life, but now I noticed things I had never seen before.

"The uniform doesn't fit him right. It's too big. Look how long the sleeves are."

"Well, as I think I mentioned, the painter probably just loaned him the uniform for his portrait."

"Nothing's right," I said scornfully. "His head is too big for his body, and look, one eye is smaller than the other."

"It was probably done by one of those traveling portrait painters. They weren't very good artists, and I guess they didn't charge much."

"He's ugly!" I said. "He's got an ugly, mean face."

"I don't know," said my aunt. "He's only about eleven or twelve, and he looks kind of thin and hungry. It really was a miserable life." She remained quiet for a moment and then said, "He became a very rich man, but nobody ever really cared for him."

"Good!" I said.

"Not even his grandson, Rafael. Gabriel brought the boy up after his mother died, but Rafael betrayed him and humiliated him. When the Americans took over California and the Presidio, Rafael served as an officer under the American flag. It just about broke the old man's heart."

"I'm glad," I said. I kept looking at the boy's face, at his dark eyes, his dark hair, and his dark skin. "I don't look anything like him," I shouted.

"No, of course you don't," said Aunt Isabel. "You look just like your mother."

"Yes," I said proudly. "I do. I want to look like my mother. But I don't want to look like him."

My aunt said, "You know, Gabriella, I've been meaning to ask you—did your mother have any family? Any brothers or sisters?"

"I don't know," I said. "She never talked about them."

"Well, I suppose we could ask Mrs. Serrano when we see her again. She might know."

I dropped my aunt's hand and looked up at her. "Why do you want to know?"

"I thought you might like to get in touch with the other side of your family. Maybe you have aunts or uncles. Wouldn't you like to find out more about your mother's family?"

"You want to get rid of me," I said angrily. "You want me to go and live with them. Isn't that what you want?"

"Now, Gabriella . . ."

"You don't want me. I remember when you said you had to take care of Grandmother because she got sick, and you wanted to have your own life again. I remember."

"Oh, Gabriella," said my aunt, pulling me over and hugging me, "you and I certainly are going to have some time working everything out, aren't we?"

"I won't," I muttered, but I leaned my head against her shoulder and stopped talking.

"Isabel! Isabel!" María shouted down the basement stairs. "You'd better come up right away. The movers are here."

"They're not supposed to come until tomorrow," said my aunt.

"Well, that's what I told them, but you'd better come and tell them yourself."

"Oh, let's go," said my aunt, putting up her hand to turn off the light.

"No, you go, Aunt Isabel. I'll come in a few minutes."

"Are you sure?"

"I'm sure, but there is one thing I want to ask you."

"What is it?"

"Well, after your grandmother died, did you ever . . .
I mean . . . did you ever see her ghost?"

"I told you, Gabriella," said my aunt firmly, "I don't
believe in ghosts."

"My father said Gabriel Valencia's ghost came to him.
Do you think he was lying?"

"*Lying* is such a hard word, Gabriella." My aunt put
a hand on my shoulder. "Maybe he really thought the
ghost came. Maybe he wanted to believe it came."

"Do you think I wanted to believe too?"

"I think you did, even though it didn't happen exactly
the way you thought it would."

"They've never come back—either one of them. But
I wouldn't mind if . . . if my mother came."

My aunt didn't say anything.

"I guess I really wanted to ask you if you . . . if you
. . . would have minded if your grandmother's ghost
came?"

"No," whispered my aunt, "I wouldn't have minded.
I would have been happy if she had, but she didn't.
Maybe it's because I never believed in ghosts, and you
have to believe in them for them to come."

We could hear some loud, angry voices upstairs, and
my aunt laughed. "We'd better go before they tear the
place apart."

"I'll be right up," I told her.

She hesitated.

"I'll be fine, Aunt Isabel. I really will."

My aunt looked worried, but the voices grew louder, and she hurried away.

When she was gone, I put my face up close to the little boy's in the portrait and said, "I'm glad Rafael was so mean to you. I'm glad he broke your heart. I hope you remembered all the horrible things you did to other people before you died, and I hope you felt scared and lonely." I gripped the frame of the painting with both my hands. "You're ugly," I sneered, "and I don't look anything like you. I'm ashamed to have you in my family, and after I go away, I'll never think of you again." I spit in the boy's face. "I'm not afraid of you," I whispered. "I don't believe anything about you, even your ghost. You can't scare me anymore."

Then I reached up and turned out the light. I began moving toward the stairs, but I heard something that made me stop. I heard—at least I thought I heard—a child crying. So I turned the light back on again and looked at him—at the awkward, clumsy little boy with spit on his face.

I tried to stop it, but it came on and grew and grew inside me. I could feel it rising, and I shook my head hard and closed my eyes. But it grew anyway—a powerful feeling of pity for him, for horrible Gabriel Valencia, for the little boy who would become a monster.

I reached out and wiped the spit off the boy's face.

Then I touched his finger, the one wearing my ring. "I won't forget you," I promised, "but I'm not going to grow up to be like you. I won't! I won't!"

Then I covered the portrait, turned out the light, and went upstairs.

Note

THE PRESIDIO OF SAN FRANCISCO was one of the oldest military bases in the United States. Founded by the Spanish in 1776, it was occupied by Mexican forces in 1822, and finally by the United States Army in 1846.

The Presidio became a national park in 1994, and is today one of the most beautiful spots in San Francisco.

Ghosts in the family /
J FIC SACHS   707922

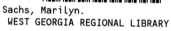

Sachs, Marilyn.
WEST GEORGIA REGIONAL LIBRARY